GYM DANDY

STORM GRANT

mlrpress

MLR PRESS AUTHORS

Featuring a roll call of some of the best writers of gay erotica and mysteries today!

Maura Anderson
Victor J. Banis
Jeanne Barrack
Laura Baumbach
Alex Beecroft
Sarah Black
Ally Blue
J.P. Bowie
P.A. Brown
James Buchanan
Jordan Castillo Price
Kit Cheng
Kirby Crow
Dick D.
Jason Edding
Angela Fiddler
Dakota Flint
Kimberly Gardner
Storm Grant
Amber Green

LB Gregg
Drewey Wayne Gunn
Samantha Kane
Kiernan Kelly
JL Langley
Josh Lanyon
Clare London
William Maltese
Gary Martine
ZA Maxfield
Jet Mykles
L. Picaro
Neil Plakcy
Luisa Prieto
AM Riley
George Seaton
Jardonn Smith
Caro Soles
Richard Stevenson
Claire Thompson

Check out titles, both available and forthcoming, at
www.mlrpress.com

GYM DANDY

STORM GRANT

mlrpress

Copyright 2009 by Storm Grant

Published by
MLR Press, LLC
3052 Gaines Waterport Rd.
Albion, NY 14411

Visit ManLoveRomance Press, LLC on the Internet:
www.mlrpress.com

Cover Art by Natalia Martinez
Cover Design by Deana C. Jamroz
Editing by Judith David
Printed in the United States of America.

ISBN# 978-1-934531-94-5

Issued 2009

DEDICATION

This book would not have been possible — indeed, my entire writing career would never have happened — without the encouragement and teachings of more people than I can possibly thank here. Just to name a few:

To Jenny Saypaw for ordering me to write, and to Chris Belfontaine for teaching me how.

To my accidental mentor, Jeffrey Round, for guiding me through the ins and outs of publishing, and to Angela Fiddler for orchestrating my introduction to MLR Press.

To my publisher, Laura Baumbach, for giving me this opportunity, and to my editor, Judith David, for making it all come together.

Thanks also to Kit Mason and Kalena for early input on this story, and to the entire online community of fan and pro writers who shared their works and their learnings over the years.

Lastly, to my real-life friends and family for their patience, encouragement, and proofreading.

Thank you all so very kindly!

Stormy

TABLE OF CONTENTS

"Well, since my body left me." Victor carried a barbell, a weight collar, and a tune across the gym, The King singing backup from the tinny ceiling speakers. Too bad Elvis always got the words wrong!

"Hey, Victor!"

"I found a new barbell." Victor ignored his boss, carrying on with his cleanup duties and his singing.

"Victor?"

Restoring the smaller items to their proper places, he turned his attention to the big weights heaped carelessly near the squat cage.

"It's down at the bend of —"

"Victor! Your four o'clock is here."

Victor acknowledged neither Phil nor his four o'clock as he hefted the last of the hundred-pound plates from squat cage to weight tree. He struggled a little as he manhandled the awkward weight toward its home. Why was it the really big muscleheads — the only ones who ever used the really big plates — were also the ones who never felt compelled to put 'em back? Certainly all the "girly-girl" weights — the fives and tens and fifteens — were neatly aligned in glossy chrome rows on the rack paralleling the wall o' mirrors. Maybe that was the trick: install a mirror over the weight trees and see if the muscleheads and the juicers would condescend to put their own frigging weights away! Victor drew a deep breath, inhaling gym funk along with a drip of sweat that slithered down his face. It tasted like mousse and gel and hairspray. And sweat.

He labored clumsily with the weight, not that it was heavy to him — hell, he could bench-press his own body weight, no problem — but the angle was just so awkward. He felt gawky and graceless as he folded his more-or-less six-foot frame into a half-squat, half-crouch, balancing the weight before him. The hole in the big plate seemed ridiculously small for the metal pole that formed the lowest branch of the weight tree; its pyramid shape did indeed resemble a pine tree — a Christmas tree even, with weight-collar angels on top.

Victor rested the plate briefly on the ground, pleased with his analogy. He heaved it up again, arms trembling, muscles drained from his own workout before his shift began. Painfully aware of being watched like TV, he labored, self-conscious of his lack of cool. A few more elastic seconds while the pole finally found the hole, and the bulky metal doughnut slid home.

Rising, slightly winded, slightly embarrassed, he muttered, "You'd think I'd be better at that, what with all the practice I've had." Checking the mirrored wall on his left, he cruised a hand across his hair; craftily gelled, it grew aggressively skyward like spiky blond turf. Satisfied, he faced his audience and winked, just to make sure no one missed his terribly clever and subtle entendre.

Holy shit! His gut clenched as he experienced a major *wow!* moment at how amazingly good-looking the new client was.

New guy was about Victor's height, hair dark and plane-smooth: the bizzaro reflection of Victor's own punky-funky, chemically enhanced blondness. Victor sometimes felt his own appeal had more to do with attitude and style than with nature being particularly kind. Four O'clock, on the other hand, had classic features and coif — he'd never go out of fashion. But then, he'd also never get picked out of a lineup to get into a really cool after-hours club. Victor could, and did on a fairly regular basis.

Reminding himself that truly handsome guys were always trouble, Victor wiped one sweaty hand on his black muscle shirt, smirking expectantly as he waited for acknowledgment of his pithy pole-in-the-hole comment.

Four O'clock just gazed at him. Great. Another live one. More evidence for Victor's half-baked hypothesis that really good-looking guys were minimalistic in the personality department.

"Victor. This is Kirk Douglas." Phil Martini, general manager and mostly sales guy of Orr's Gym, passed the new guy's paperwork to Victor like an Olympic torch — one that had served its purpose and was now sputtering out.

The familiarly named Kirk Douglas coughed nervously, politely covering his mouth with his left hand, extending his right, "That would be Douglas Newkirk, actually. Please call me Doug." Looking slightly uncomfortable, he glanced sideways at Phil, as if correcting the manager du jour of downtown Toronto's Orr's Gym franchise constituted a major social gaffe.

Victor juggled the clipboard to free one hand, successfully regaining his client's attention. "Victor Brighton." He introduced himself and gripped the guy's hand a few warm moments, releasing it before it got awkward.

"It's a pleasure to meet you, sir."

Victor was impressed. Very few people here ever called him 'sir'. He smiled at the new member. Phil gave a *gotta-go* cough, which Victor acknowledged with an *I'll take it from here* nod without taking his eyes off Newkirk.

Phil started off, but turned back for a second. "Hey, Victor. Ms. Amorotique wants to see you after your shift tomorrow. *Time for your six-week review.*" He sing-songed the latter as he made tracks for the elevator, no doubt headed back to the front desk to make another sale. He'd got this Douglas guy's credit card, so he was done with him. Victor wouldn't be surprised if Phil's middle name was "commission."

The ball was now firmly in Victor's court. He studied the clipboard, scratching behind one ear with his worn-down pencil.

He took his job seriously, even though management was pretty ambivalent about whether a member stayed on or not. They seemed to feel that showing the ropes to new members was largely a farce. Victor had been told during his one hour of training that the gym actually made more profit on people who paid their dues and then disappeared.

That's not what the fitness industry wanted people to think, though. *We're dedicated to your success!* they all claimed. One all-women gym downtown even promised wake-up calls for morning workouts and incentive calls if you didn't show for a couple of weeks. *Hah!* Sit by the phone and wait, girlfriend. They ain't never gonna call. They also promised the lowest rates in town — for the crappiest equipment and tiniest facility. If the sign-me-up-quick, bargain-greedy, no-pain-just-gain, wishful-thinking, deliberately misled consumer only knew...

Where was I again? New guy. Right. Right. Vic studied the clipboard like he was back in school it would count for 50% of his final mark.

Each new member was asked a series of personally tailored questions and given a custom program — not! The same questions for everybody, the same custom program: guy, girl, young, old, fat, thin. Made no difference. The printout said this guy wanted to lose weight and get in shape. Christ, who didn't? Okay, Victor could work with that.

He shifted his focus from clipboard to client. "Okay, um..." Oh, shit. He'd forgotten the guy's name already. McDougall was it? No, something Douglas. A sly peek at the paperwork, "Doug. Let's have a look at you." Vic stalked around Doug in a protracted arc, peering at front, side, back, then front again. Doug's sweat suit was baggy and unflattering, with some kind of faded crest on the sweatshirt...post office, maybe? Victor stared at the new guy's front so long that Doug began fidgeting, cheap running shoes squeaking with newness. He finally clasped his hands in front, small gym towel obscuring his crotch completely. Bright red towel, eh? Nelly must be behind on the gym's laundry again.

Victor ran his professional gaze back up the somewhere-around-six-feet of Doug's body, spending way too much time on the fine-looking face. The guy had a faint discoloration on his sculpted jawline, a fading purple-green shiner that clashed badly with the dark blue eyes, and a small cut in one eyebrow that would probably scar. Good. A scar would be a nice contrast with the matinée idol looks — go a long way toward making him more approachable. Probably thought he was hot

Heading back toward the staircase, Victor stopped and looked around, taking a deep sniff. "Mmmm. Love that really old building smell, eh?" Victor sucked air, noticing Doug's flared nostrils and horse-about-to-bolt look. "I think it's a national monument or something."

"It's not actually been approved by the Historical Society of Greater Toronto yet, but I believe an application has been made." Doug shifted the thirty-pound dumbbell to his other hand, resting it on the staircase railing.

"And you would know this because…?"

"Why, because I did the research before I decided to join this particular fitness establishment." His look said, "Wouldn't anyone?"

"So to decide which gym to join, you check out the building? That's very…um, thorough. Yeah, thorough. I like that. You're a thorough kind of guy. Me, now, if I had to research every single decision like that, I'd die from boredom before I got in a single rep."

"Actually, I think you'd find this particular building has a fascinating history. It was erected in the early part of the last century, originally as a government office. If you stand outside on the sidewalk and look up, as I did before entering, you'll see the building has maintained some outstanding architectural details, such as the pillared stone railing rimming the balcony on the uppermost floor."

"Did I say something funny?"

"You said *rim*… Never mind. Go on with the history lesson." Victor cut the *heh heh* noises. It made him sound like a dirty old man, anyway. But who worked *rimming* into a conversation? This was getting interesting.

The history lesson continued for some minutes. "And finally, you'll notice that above the main entrance on Isabella Street, gargoyles, eroded by time, painted by pigeons, still stand guard on the concrete façade."

"Hey. That's better than the Discovery Channel. Where'd you find out all this stuff?" He fiddled with the hole where his earring usually was — no stud today.

Doug spoke of a number of Web sites where you could investigate business, architecture, health and fitness.

"The Internet, you say." Victor scratched his stubbled chin, the stairway's fluorescent light painting a scruffy halo against his jawline. "I'll have to check that out one of these days."

※ ※ ※

As they returned to the top floor, Victor surveyed his workplace anew, trying to see it through Doug's eyes. He'd already figured Doug for the observant type; he'd make a hell of a witness. Doug hadn't mentioned it, but Victor was fairly certain he, too, had noted the second-rate interior renovations done to the place. Money had been poured into the fancy reception area; it made promises of style that the rest of the gym just couldn't keep. The prefab walls throughout wore builder's beige, scarring easily each time a weight thunked against one. Twelve-foot ceilings bared their pipes and ductwork and were covered in a hideous spray-on foam that was supposed to provide sound dampening. Unfortunately, it just looked like thick gray fungus growing over the entire ceiling. Victor shuddered and looked at the floor instead.

Victor noticed, not for the first time, the way the carpeting curled and lifted where the polyester squares were gradually losing their grip. The tweedy-gray texture didn't really do much to hide the stains and ghosts of leaks past.

He inhaled deeply. While the basement had smelled of locker rooms and forgotten sneakers, the three other floors smelled uniformly of mildew, warm vinyl and, depending on the immediate mix of clientele, perfume, cologne, hair care products, and steroid-laced sweat. The weights and equipment lent that metallic smell of iron and steel, although how metal could smell was a mystery to Victor. Sometimes it seemed the gym was rife with iron-y smell.

Victor rambled on about health and fitness as he and Doug toured their way through all four floors, ending up back where they'd started, on top. Dutifully, Doug lugged the thirty-pound dumbbell with him every step of the way, including up and down stairs since Victor had bypassed the elevator. "Stairs count as aerobic activity, don't you know?" he'd cheerfully informed his new client.

"Got any questions at this point, Kirk — Curt — Doug?" Victor corrected himself. He really needed to learn this guy's name, although a tiny voice in the back of his mind suggested *babe* or some other term of endearment. Mentally, he bitch-slapped the tiny voice into submission.

"Yes, actually. I do." Doug gestured half-heartedly with the dumbbell, panting a little. His candy-pink tongue slipped out to run along his upper lip, replacing the damp sheen of sweat with a wee hint of saliva. For just a moment, Victor was the mongoose, hypnotized by Doug's cobra-like tongue.

Which Doug was currently using to ask, "When will we be employing this weight I've been carrying?"

"Getting heavy?" Victor waited patiently for the response, gaze sharp and expectant on Doug.

"A little." Doug ran his tongue across his lower lip now. "It's only thirty pounds, after all." Balancing it on his thigh, he shifted the weight to just one hand. He gingerly flexed the cramped fingers of the now-free hand, the criss-cross knurl pattern clearly embossing his palm.

"Yeah, but after a while, carrying thirty extra pounds around gets pretty exhausting. A pretty inconvenient pain in the ass, right?" Victor cocked his head slightly to one side and waited for his new client to get it.

Waiting…

Doug maintained eye contact, but eventually dropped his gaze.

Waiting…

Doug switched hands again, fingering the stitches in his eyebrow.

Waiting...

"Oh. I see what you mean. I'm carrying an extra thirty pounds of subcutaneous fat around with me and you're saying I'll feel much better without it."

"Bingo!" Got it in one. "That's exactly my point. And to extrapo...eluci...elaborate, I'm also saying that joining a gym is not the magic answer to all your problems." Damn, he'd wanted to impress Doug with his vocabulary since Doug's own was obviously huge, but he'd ended up stumbling over the big words instead. Victor figured he'd better stick to things he was good at from now on. Luckily, there were some things he was very good at and maybe he could impress Doug with those instead.

He focused on Doug, who was giving him another skeptical look. "No. See," Victor answered, though Doug hadn't asked, "you'd be surprised how many people figure once they've paid their membership fees, they've paid their dues, if you know what I mean."

Doug's body language still read *unconvinced*. Victor pushed some more. He was certainly good at this. At making people come to the conclusions he wanted them to, at making people reveal more of themselves than they realized they were. He'd spent a lifetime learning how.

"It's not enough to give money to some gym; you have to also give blood, sweat and tears. Well, mainly sweat." Victor zapped his new protégé with his laser beam smile. He was pretty sure already that Doug would be one of the few that stayed, who achieved a measure of success. He seemed like a very determined guy. Plus, Victor wanted to see him again.

"And you can't just work out with weights and machines. You have to get some aerobic exercise, too. Hell, half the muscleheads — the really big guys — who come in here five times a week are actually in pretty shitty shape. Especially if they're juicing it."

"Excuse me?"

"You know. Juice. 'Roids."

Vic rolled his eyes as Doug said "Huh?"

"An-a-bol-ic ster-oids," Victor enunciated clearly, keeping his voice low. He surveyed the room, praying no one heard him filling in the new guy. He'd get in royal shit if that got back to either the users or the boss lady. The local cops were onto it, of course; even suspected Orr's was a major depot for illegal steroids and human growth hormone — not just the synthetic crap, but, if you had the coin, the real stuff harvested from human cadavers. And not always healthy cadavers, either…if a cadaver could be…

Victor refocused on Doug, who was saying, "There are individuals working out here who employ performance-enhancing pharmaceuticals?" Doug looked appalled. And was speaking way too loud.

Victor grabbed Doug's elbow and dragged him over into the corner behind the ab crunch machine, taking the dumbbell from him and replacing it on its designated rack as they passed. "Shhhh. We don't discuss stuff like that out in the open. Okay?" He lowered his voice, speaking up a bit as they stepped directly below a ceiling speaker. Some '80s pop diva was scratchily belting out a techno-ballad. Orr's really needed to invest in a better sound system.

Doug nodded and ran one thumb down his nose. Victor got it instantly, returning the sly gesture. "Yeah. Steroid use is a whole hell of a lot more common than people think. Especially in a hardcore bodybuilder gym like this one."

Doug's gaze jumped suspiciously from one to the next of the gym's current patrons, those few people lucky enough to get in their training before the afterwork rush began. "Perhaps I have joined the wrong gymnasium. I'm under the impression I have thirty days to change my mind and pay on a pro rata basis for only those days that have passed since joining. Perhaps you could recommend a more suitable establishment for me, then. Or would that put you in an awkward position professionally?"

"Jeez, Doug." Victor clenched and released Doug's bicep. When had he grabbed his upper arm? And why the hell had he brought any of this up? Doug was so obviously not the kind of guy who had any info on steroids. "I didn't mean to scare you off. Just show you the ropes. Don't worry 'bout it. There's never any trouble here, leastways, not very often. And besides, steroid use is pretty universal — you're going to find it in any gym or health club you join. It's even in high schools, for Chrissake."

Victor was seriously worried he'd lose this client and get in shit with Phil and the boss; Ms. Amorotique seemed pretty tough. And he really needed to stay working here, at this particular gym. "Look, I got way off on a tangent here. What I wanted to say is that you need to do more than just come in here three times a week and haul chunks of metal around. You need to incorporate some aerobic exercise into your workouts, too. No. No. Not aerobics classes per se. Those aren't for everybody. Besides, they charge extra for 'em. I'm thinking stationary bicycle or stair climber. Or treadmill. Whatever. They got a few downstairs in the aerobics area, but you have to get here at off-hours to get a turn on them. They're usually signed up well in advance. Oh, yeah. And they charge extra for them, too."

Victor watched as Doug's gaze ran appraisingly over his own well-defined, whipcord body. He'd never make the cover of *Muscle Mag;* more like some fitness and health rag, maybe. He leaned back in his stance a bit so his torso was properly showcased, knowing the black spandex bike shorts made the best of his long, long legs. Pirouette, plié, laugh to cover the twinge of insecurity at this handsome guy's scrutiny. Well, turnabout's fair play, right? He'd stared his fill earlier, strictly professional, of course. Plus you really have to consider the source of any fitness advice you're given. So let the guy look. If Victor played his cards right, maybe they could see a whole lot more of each other later.

"What do you do for aerobic exercise, if I may inquire, Mr. Brighton?"

"Mr. Brighton?" Victor had been expecting the question, but not the formality. "That's, like, my dad or something. Call me Victor, 'kay?" That taken care of, he answered the actual question. "I box. I dance. I…" He'd been going to say, "I fuck." It was his stock reply to this inevitable question, and tended to get a nervous laugh, or sometimes a welcome invitation. But for whatever reason, he couldn't say this to Doug.

"Yes, Victor? You…?"

"I…run." Quick save. Brilliant save.

"Running, *hmmm*. I used to run a bit. When there weren't several feet of snow on the ground. I'm from up north — Northern Ontario." Doug gestured toward the water fountain, presumably indicating the north side of the building. And of Canada. "I think I could take up running again."

"Running, yeah. Good idea. But now, let's *run* through your custom designed workout developed exclusively for you by highly trained professionals." Victor was mighty good at pretending — his job depended on it.

He led Doug to his first station.

※ ※ ※

Victor spent the next hour putting Doug through the standard "custom" workout, although he did personalize it a bit after Doug said he couldn't put too much strain on his back due to a recent injury, one he didn't wish to elaborate on even at Victor's insistence.

They were almost done when a swarthy, well-cut young man came onto the floor wearing the same black muscle shirt as Victor. Unlike Victor, however, this guy had ripped out the sleeves, enlarged the neck and cut off the bottom till there was scarcely enough material left to contain the word *Staff* screenprinted across the back in bright red. "Hey, Vic," he called in greeting. "Weren't you off shift half an hour ago?"

"Yeah, Gus. Yeah. Just finishing up with the new guy, here." He nodded toward Doug as he put away the last of their free weights.

Doug finished his final set on the leg press rather faster than Victor had demonstrated. "Oh, dear. I certainly didn't intend to keep you after hours on my account. Will you be compensated for the overtime?"

With his back to Doug, Victor used the mirror in front of him to see Doug behind him. It was a habit most gym rats picked up, and sorely missed when they were out in the real world and had to look directly at things. Doug seemed genuinely upset. A few other bored lifters stared at them intrusively, no doubt hoping for some entertainment between sets. Lifting large pieces of metal over and over could only hold your attention for so long.

"Nah. Not a problem, though. I wouldn't have left you hanging." He grabbed his faded and frayed black towel and headed for the exit. "Shift's over. Workout's done. Let's go." Doug followed dutifully as he had for the last hour and a half.

As they headed down the stairs they crossed paths with a group of young men in extreme muscle shirts and outrageously baggy shorts ringed with peeking-out designer underwear. The lead guy, a camo do-rag over his hair, sang out, "Hey, Victor," the tone mocking. "Or should I say *Vicky*?" The buddies on the stairs laughed meanly. "Butthole surfer," he jeered under his breath.

Victor paused for just a second, then seriously, coldly, deadly: "That would be *Mister* Surfer to you, Levon."

A few nervous chuckles from the other boys, obviously uncertain exactly who to root for now that Victor had failed to rise to their ringleader's bait.

Victor continued down the stairs, ignoring Levon and crew — but just a step past the mocking boy he reached back and yanked off the scarf.

Protesting loudly, Levon tried to cover his hair, which was squashed and flatted from the headgear. "Fuck you!" he yelled, obviously pissed that his homies were now laughing at *him* rather than at his intended target.

Victor tossed him the scarf; Levon fumbled and nearly dropped it. Cackling and pushing, his friends moved him bodily away from any possible confrontation and on toward their evening workout.

Victor shook his head, trying an avuncular chuckle that didn't quite sit right. Off duty now, Victor didn't really feel inclined to deal with Doug, who, on the stairs behind him, looked stricken at the insulting byplay. Victor continued on his way downstairs.

When he reached the lowest level, he jerked open the door to the musty change room with a bit too much force. It whumped noisily on the cement-block wall behind him. The tips of his ears pinked up a bit at this display of pique he didn't want anyone to see. He moved quickly across the room, and, with a few precise movements, he opened his lock and locker. He stripped, grabbed a larger but no less scruffy towel and showered, ever vigilant of getting his artfully spiked hair wet, aware he was just as vain about his own "do" as young Levon.

He emerged a few minutes later, surprised to find Doug, changed into blue jeans and a plaid shirt, waiting for him by his locker. Well, well. The plot thickens. He was glad to have something to take his mind off that ungrateful young bastard on the stairs.

He noticed Doug holding his wallet in both hands, bills peeking out from the shadowed interior.

"What?" Victor asked, suspicious and maybe a little paranoid.

"Well, um. I feel I must compensate you for the overtime you put in on my behalf." Doug kept his eyes focused on the worn, brown leather wallet, turning it over and over in his hands. "So if you would just be so kind as to suggest an appropriate dollar figure, I'd, ah…" For a fraction of a second, Doug had looked directly at Victor, then whipped his focus back to the wallet again as if it could answer the question itself. Was he blushing?

Oh. Right. New guy. Not used to a lot of bare-ass nudity. Victor realized the towel he carried in his hand might have been more wisely wrapped around his waist. Another gym rat habit, parading around naked in the change room: *Looky what I got.* He reached across his chest to scratch the old tattoo that had decorated his bicep since long before they were trendy.

"Forget it, Doug." He grabbed his Calvin Klein boxers and pulled them on as efficiently as possible over still damp skin. They bunched around his thighs, and his temporary lack of grace made him wish Doug was looking somewhere else. Oh, wait. He was. Great.

Doug had put the wallet away and was now searching for the secrets of the universe in the bank of lockers along the left wall. Victor watched as Doug tried turning his back completely to Victor but swung immediately toward the lockers again. Victor guessed Doug had noticed the huge, full-length mirror blanketing the rear wall. Mirrors were one thing the gym hadn't skimped on.

"Well, then. You must at least allow me to buy you dinner, then." For one surreal second, it seemed like Doug was asking the lockers to dinner. "That is, of course, if you're not busy. I mean. Well, that's certainly presumptuous of me. Of course, you must have plans. Well, I just thought that…"

For a few moments, Victor let his inner bad guy savor the spectacle of Doug struggling to ask him out. It was petty of him, but he couldn't help himself and briefly enjoyed this revenge against all the beautiful people who'd rejected him over the years. He was a fast wallower, though, and felt adequately avenged before Doug had even finished speaking.

"I'm sure that someone like you must have dozens of —"

"Okay." Victor interrupted.

Doug's head snapped around to face Victor, saw him making final adjustments to his briefs — to what was in his briefs, to be specific — then whiplashed away so fast Victor feared for Doug's cervical safety. Victor ran a mental review of his first aid training: asphyxiation, bleeding, broken neck. Check. What was with this guy?

"Okay?"

"Yeah. I said okay. What part of *o* and *kay* don't you get?"

"Yes. Well, then. What are you hungry for?"

Hmmm, what indeed? Victor let his gaze travel up Doug's body. The jeans were certainly an improvement over the crappy sweats. He pulled on his own black jeans as he pondered the question. "There's a new Thai place on Church." Safe bet. There was always a new Thai place on Church.

"That sounds like an excellent choice. I don't believe I've had Thai food before, although certainly everyone seems to…I'll just wait outside, then. Right you are." Doug fled Victor's side just as a colossal naked man emerged from the showers.

Victor snickered at the spectacle that was Doug Newkirk's hasty departure. Trying to head directly to the exit without looking at the other men in the change room, Doug careened off the freestanding bank of lockers, rebounded against the privacy wall and managed to catch his gym bag on the door handle on his way through. Victor shook his head hard; had Doug just apologized to the wall?

The locker room door closed on the strap of Doug's gym bag, then it slowly creaked open again as a disembodied hand reached back in to liberate the trapped strap.

Still sniggering faintly, Victor nodded to the large and powerful-looking man now toweling off, one foot braced on the bench not far from Victor's ass. Victor pulled on his other boot. "Hey, Danny."

"Jeez, Vic. You sure can pick 'em. He's pretty enough, but I hope he's less clumsy in the sack."

"Yeah. Me, too." Victor stood to zip up. Checking the mirror one more time, he decided his hair was spiked to his liking, slung his gym bag over his shoulder, and headed out to find the promising Douglas Newkirk.

THAI ME UP, THAI ME DOWN

Exiting the gym at the Isabella entrance, Victor spied his dinner companion waiting off to one side. The late afternoon sunshine highlighted his hair blue-gold where he leaned hipshot against the probably-not-very-clean façade of the building. A brown leather gym bag rested on the sidewalk beside him. Victor wondered if the matching gym bag, leather jacket, hiking boots and wallet were deliberate, or if Doug was just a monochromatic kind of guy.

"Is the restaurant far?" Doug asked.

"Nah. We'll walk. This way." Victor led them across the parking lot, hopped over the low fence, and started down a muddy laneway behind a row of old houses. Doug, looking increasingly nervous, followed slowly.

They ended up in the backyard of a deserted building. It looked like it had once been residential, but had been boarded up and awaited demolition. Victor had discovered this "free" parking spot on his second day with Orr's and now parked there daily. No way was he paying $35 a day to park his car for a job that paid hardly more than that. That would just look weird. Victor tossed his gym bag into the trunk.

"Dump your gear and we'll walk over to Church Street." Vic jittered while Doug hesitated. Victor had never been known for his patience, and quickly grew antsy. He solved their immediate problem by reaching over and yanking Doug's bag from his shoulder and dropping it beside his own. Banging the trunk closed, he pretended not to hear Doug's "But perhaps I'd better…"

"We'll pick the stuff up on the way back. No point lugging it around, right?" He moved to the passenger side. "I just got to check something for a sec. 'Kay?" Opening the door, he leaned in, grabbed what he needed from the glove compartment, the metal on metal clinking audibly, and shoved it into the inside pocket of his black leather jacket before Doug noticed.

Doug appeared to be memorizing his license plate. He shifted uneasily. "Nice car, Victor. Are you a classic car aficionado?"

"What?" Victor patted his faded jeans, ensuring his wallet had made the transition from his gym bag to his pocket.

Tugging at one ear, Doug elaborated, "This car. Are you fixing it up?" He indicated the partially restored classic T-bird, dotted with puke-colored body filler.

"Yeah. I'm into the classics." Doug's earlier sentence had finally caught up with him. "But that ain't mine." He hooked his thumb over his shoulder toward the T-bird as they started away from the surrogate parking lot. "This is just a loaner from the body shop. My car's being detailed. My baby's a Goat," he said proudly.

"Ahhhh. I understand completely." Doug said. "So you have children, then?"

"What?" Victor echoed his earlier comment, starting to worry that his companion would think him an idiot. Or vice versa. "My ex-wife didn't want children, so I don't have any...as far as I know..." Instead of the standard nudge, nudge, wink, wink, his sentence trailed off uncertainly. How did they get on the subject of children?

"I must confess, however, that I'm unclear as to why you would say your baby is a goat if you have no children. Do you keep livestock, then?"

Victor's turn to *ahhhh*. "No. No. Doug. My car is a 'Goat.' A GTO. Get it? No? Okay, I'll explain. A Pontiac GTO is sometimes called a Goat."

Doug thumbed his injured eyebrow again. Victor seized his hand, stopping them both on the sidewalk and arresting the thumb mid arc.

"Cut that out. You'll get those stitches infected or something."

"Ah. Sorry." He gradually lowered their joined hands. "Nervous habit, I'm afraid." Time stopped. (Though not for the crabby couple whose path they were blocking.) Victor felt lost and disoriented as he stared into Doug's gorgeous dark blue eyes.

Doug drew back his hand slowly. The spell shattered. Victor watched Doug look anywhere but at him. Wordlessly, they continued their amble along Isabella Street.

"Ah," Doug said for the third time in as many minutes. The conversation deteriorated from there. Victor couldn't imagine spending the evening in uncomfortable silence with a relative stranger, so, when in doubt, let it out. And said exactly that.

"You know, Douggie, I've never been good at making small talk. Yolanda — that's my ex — used to get all bent out of shape about it. Said I was fucking up her career." He noticed Doug flinch at the coarse language. Was this guy a priest or something? He sure hoped not. Or maybe...

"And besides," Victor carried on, "It's mostly boring anyway. To both of us. So why don't I just stop trying to be polite and start asking you stuff that interests me and you start talking about stuff that interests you? And if either of us gets too personal, we just say so. No farm, no fowl. Right?"

"Victor, I don't think that's quite the..."

Victor's smirk must have made him reconsider. Doug drew a breath and began what could have been any number of habitual gestures, but clasped his hands securely behind his back instead. "Well, it does seem that your...approach to conversation will guarantee a more enjoyable evening for you. And since this is, in theory, repayment for your valuable time, I will endeavor to be as entertaining as I can."

"You always talk like that? You a professor or something?"

"No. I'm an accountant, actually. I spend a lot of time behind a desk, which may account..." He smiled at his weak joke. "For my progressive weight gain over the years."

"But you didn't get that shiner from being an accountant. You get mugged?"

"Well, actually, I —"

Any response to Victor's eloquent *huh?* was cut short by their arrival at the restaurant.

There was indeed a new Thai place over on Church: Thai One On was the far too clever name of the eatery du jour. Victor tried to recall how many different restaurants had been through there over the last few years, but failed to come up with a single one, and also failed to care.

The décor was every bit as clever as the name, uniting the de rigueur souvenirs of Thailand with Canadian memorabilia in an inelegant mix. A plastic pagoda leaned precariously against a small CN Tower, hopelessly out of scale with each other. A whiskery oriental dragon battled a taxidermed beaver above the bar. It was an interior decorator's nightmare, and in no way explained the Garfield-the-cat phone on which the host spoke loudly in some language that may or may not have been Thai. He yelled what sounded to Victor like *"Pang muk muk,"* and smacked down the phone. "Table for two, guys?" he asked in accent-free English, switching on a toothy smile from a dentist's wet dream.

Even though it was not quite seven, the place was fairly busy. Must be date night; all the two- and four-seaters were taken. The maître d' sat them in a circular booth that could probably have accommodated Bob Marley and all of The Wailers — who were currently serenading the guests on the restaurant's jukebox, ensuring cultural overload for all.

Once settled, Victor leapt back into interrogation mode. "You said you got mugged? What happened? Are you okay?"

Doug stared at him blankly a moment. "No..." he started slowly. "Perhaps I wasn't clear. I'm afraid my injuries were sustained as a result of my work as an accountant."

"No shit?" Again Doug gave that strange little flinch. "What did you do? Report somebody for tax evasion or something?"

He leaned across the table to lay a hand gently on Doug's forearm. "You okay?" he repeated.

By touching Doug, it seemed to Victor that he'd arrested time again. He would have been content to stroke Doug's arm lightly and gaze into his blue, blue eyes forever. He finally drew back his hand as the neo-Goth waitress approached. Pulling a grubby notebook from the waistband of her black vintage skirt, she asked, "What'll you have, boys?"

Their ordered was delayed, however, when the pen she'd stored behind one multi-pierced ear became entangled in her jewellery. Victor leapt to the rescue and soon it was free.

"No problem." He winked charmingly. "Got a piercing of my own." Her kohl rimmed eyes crinkled when she smiled. Back in waitress mode, she asked, "Drinks, guys? Food?"

They ordered green tea and pad Thai, Doug following Victor's more knowledgeable lead. Their waitress, whose name, according to the inscription on the gold plastic name badge, was KiKi, returned shortly and clattered two chipped Chinese-style cups on the table. The many layers of white plastic tablecloth cushioned the impact. "Oops," she giggled, and placed the pot, inexplicably shaped like a duck, between them.

"I like this green tea stuff, but I'm not big on regular tea. More of a coffee man, myself." Victor announced. Raising the tea duck, he poured a few drops into his Blue Willow knock-off cup to check the color. A puddle of brownish-yellow pooled on the plastic beneath the teapot's bill like so much duck drool.

"Not steep enough yet." He felt rather worldly, introducing Doug to this new experience. He wondered what other experiences Doug might like to share with him.

Still toying with the tea things, Victor took up the cross-examination again. "So if it's not too personal, explain to me how being an accountant gets you beat up like that." Victor gently grasped Doug's chin, turning his head so the light from the jolly paper lanterns illuminated the bruises in all their Technicolor splendor.

Doug looked uneasy but allowed Victor to manipulate his head from side to side, twitching under the scrutiny like a prize stallion. Sensing he was about to bolt, Victor let go. "Well?"

Doug fiddled with the little wooden chopsticks. "The particular branch of accounting I practice is known as forensic accounting." Doug paused as if this were adequate explanation.

"Okay, Doug. I get *forensic*. And I get *accounting*. What I don't get is *forensic accounting*. I thought forensics was all about fingerprints and DNA and stuff like that." Actually, he knew a fair amount about forensics, and was interested to learn more. He did the "girl thing," looking all innocent and impressed.

Doug seemed delighted with his audience; was it possible he didn't get much chance to talk about his job? "That is indeed a large part of forensics, but by no means all of it. Forensic accounting involves the analysis of activities through paperwork, and, in the last few decades, computers. It's often used to improve systems, identify areas for business simplification, find accounting errors."

Maybe this wasn't the most fascinating lecture on forensics ever. Victor tapped a jittery tattoo on the plastic tablecloth using air-band magic to convert chopsticks into drumsticks. He scrutinized the room, craned his neck to re-read the specials, checked out the other patrons.

"It's also used to solve crimes, identify malfeasants, and provide irrefutable evidence in court."

"Solve crimes, eh?" Doug had Victor's undivided attention now.

"Tell me about that. I'm, er, a big fan of those reality TV cop shows. That how you got the shiner?"

"Yes. I work freelance. That seems to be the best arrangement for all concerned. Somehow I don't seem to fit into the normal office environment." Victor thought he could see why — this guy was smart, funny, good-looking. Yeah. Who'd want him around?

"I have often been attached to various law enforcement agencies, including the RCMP."

"You're a Mountie, then? Where's the hat?"

Doug flushed and paled simultaneously, which was no mean feat. "Ah, no. But when I was young, I thought I might make a career with the RCMP." He ran a tongue halfway across his lower lip, intent on folding his cheap paper napkin just so. "Or the NHL."

The long pause was telling; Victor made a mental note to first, not pry into people's personal lives that were none of his business, and, second, to get the whole story as soon as possible.

Before Victor's patience cracked, which wasn't long at all, Doug continued. "I'm often sent into areas of criminal activity — usually after the initial arrests have been made and proof is needed for evidentiary purposes. Over the years, I've been retained by a number of government agencies."

"Like for instance?"

"For instance the Canada Revenue Agency, the Receiver General's office, the Ontario Provincial Police, and the RCMP. I've also done work for Wackenhutt, Brinks and several other private security firms."

"Wackenhutt. *Heh, heh.* See, that just sounds funny."

Doug frowned. "They're a security firm, Victor."

Victor collected himself. "That's a pretty impressive résumé, Doug, but you're not enlightening me any about these." Victor ran a gentle finger down Doug's temple, where the worst of the rainbow contusions dappled his pretty face. Doug drew back a little, tapping on the table twice with his fingertips as KiKi-the-waitress refreshed their tea.

"It means *thank you* in certain parts of Asia. I'm not sure about Thailand, but it never hurts to err on the side of politeness."

"Doug, she's as Canadian as we are. She couldn't find Thailand on a map even with both Rand and McNally helping her."

Doug shifted in his seat, the aging red vinyl creaking faintly. "Be that as it may."

Oops. Doug almost looked like he was going to sulk. Men. Can't live with 'em. Can't shoot 'em. "Sorry, Doug. You were saying?" Victor poured a little tea into his cup. "Okay. It's so steep you need a ladder now." He poured first for Doug, then filled his own to the brim.

After taking a test sip, Doug drained the cup and held it out for more. As Victor refilled it and reached for his own, Doug took up the tale again.

"This time was a bit different. The RCMP had suspicions about the nature of certain business dealings of an individual. I can't tell you his name or specific details, as his trial is still pending."

"So they sent you in undercover. That it?" Victor jumped ahead, trying to read the final chapter before the story could unfold.

"Yes. I was provisionally deputized as an officer of the court, and sent in to act as temporary replacement for an ailing bookkeeper."

"Except he wasn't ailing, was he? He was under arrest for something and agreed to be a witness for the Crown. Right?"

Doug looked surprised by Victor's leap of logic.

But the story was further delayed as KiKi arrived with their pad Thai and chicken satay with bean sprouts.

"But, Miss. I'm afraid we didn't order any —"

"Yeah, well, the kitchen got the orders mixed up. Again." She looked very tired, her raccoon eyes red as well as blue and black. "The cook's Thai — *surprise!* — and his English isn't so good. And my Thai-ish sucks." She shifted from Doc Marten to Doc Marten, snuck a peek at the Garfield-talking owner, leaned in and whispered, "I'll put it on the bill at the price of pad Thai. Cashews are killer expensive."

"Hey, thanks. We'll take it." Victor knew a bargain when he saw one. To her offer to get them anything else, Victor said, "I'm going to use chopsticks, but I think my friend here needs a fork." Victor planned to impress Doug with his knowledge of international cuisine, but Doug informed them that chopsticks would be fine.

Doug proceeded to use his chopsticks with skill that would have impressed Mr. Miyagi. Victor was good, but not that good. "Thought you'd never had Thai before," Victor accused, competitively transferring sprouts from plate to mouth, losing most of them in his haste.

"I haven't, but I was practically raised on Chinese food. My grandparents were involved with a world literacy organization most of their working lives. At one point before I was born, they were stationed in the Fuchow region of China. They developed a certain fondness for Chinese culture, often preparing traditional Chinese dishes once they'd moved back to Canada. It was necessary from time to time for them to substitute one food item for another. For instance, we often had Mandarin-style moose, partridge fried rice —"

"That how you learned about the chopsticks?"

"Well, these chopsticks are rather different from either Chinese or Japanese, so it's no wonder you're having some difficulty. Here, you hold them like so…" Doug slid around the booth until they were shoulder to shoulder, gently wrapping his fingers over Victor's to demonstrate the proper grip.

"Like this, Doug?" Victor fumbled, dropping the shrimp for the third time. "Show me again." Coy. He could do coy. And not the pond variety, either.

Doug's touch was rapidly becoming more determined than gentle, as he manipulated Victor's fingers yet again.

"Like this, then." The moment for fake ineptitude over, Victor swiped a particularly fine chunk of chicken from Doug's plate with practiced dexterity. Doug gave him a frown of disapproval. Uh, oh. Busted.

"Look, Victor!" Doug cried, pointing toward the back of the restaurant. "A Goat!"

Victor swung his head back just in time to see Doug down the last shrimp of the evening — one that had previously rested atop Victor's diminishing heap of pad Thai.

Doug grinned victoriously, the ass-end of the shrimp protruding from his sauce-slick lips. Victor reached up and pinched the tail as Doug applied his sharp, slightly uneven teeth to sever it from the body. Victor tossed the tail cavalierly over his shoulder into a dusty plastic palm tree with pressed maple leaves hot-glued to its trunk. Go figure. Laughter freckled the tablecloth with bits of shrimp and chicken.

"So this accountant guy." Victor had recovered enough to prod for further details. "He cut a deal with the Crown to rat on his boss, and they sent you in as his replacement?"

"That's essentially correct. Arrangements were made with an agency in the business of supplying temporary accounting clerks to send me in as the other fellow's replacement, saying he'd set this up just before taking emergency leave."

"So he's out and you're under deep cover, just like *Miami Vice*."

"Miami vice? The RCMP does have a vice division, but it's headquartered in Ottawa. I realize many Canadians choose to winter in Florida, hence the term *snowbirds*, but what has Miami got to do with it?"

"No. No. See *Miami Vice* was a… Never mind. Just finish the undercover story, and after that you can tell me exactly what planet you're from where they don't have radio or TV or senses of humor or anything."

Doug looked slightly taken aback, but Victor smiled winningly, doing that head-tilting thing that had once caused him to look up *winsome* in the dictionary. It had been defined as "engaging" and "appealing," and must have worked, because Doug looked somewhat mollified.

"There's not much left to the story. I worked at this organization for several weeks — long enough to unearth enough concrete evidence of criminal activity to put the principal and most of his management team away for some time. On my last day there, I worked late into the night; everyone else was long gone. I e-mailed all the necessary records to my contact at RCMP headquarters using a virtual mailbox —"

"What's a virtual —"

"Like Hotmail," Doug elaborated. "To make it that much harder for the suspects to trace if they became suspicious. I was just packing up the last of the hardcopy to take away with me; I'd taken a little home with me each evening, claiming I wanted to work on it some more before the next business day. They were a bit wary at first, but when I behaved very much in the manner of a man who is desperate to make a good impression in order to secure a permanent position —"

"You kissed a lot of management butt, you mean."

"In a manner of speaking, yes. But as I was leaving that last day, it became apparent that management was, as they say, on to me. I was apprehended on my way to the bus stop, and beaten about the head and shoulders by two henchmen with blunt objects. I believe one had a baseball bat and one a two-by-four. They left me unconscious in a parking lot."

"Jesus, Doug. How long ago was that? Are you sure you should be working out yet? Did they catch the guys who did it?"

Doug placed his crumpled paper napkin beside his empty plate. "That was almost six weeks ago. And I appreciate your concern, but I assure you I'm fine now. The doctors have given me a clean bill of health and I'm anxious to begin a fitness regimen, although I'm not quite sure this dinner should be part of my diet." He frowned at his grease-shiny plate and stroked his slightly rounded stomach. "And yes, I'm glad to say that medical forensic evidence — that's the kind of thing you see more of on television shows, and yes, I do, on occasion, watch television — was instrumental in identifying the men who attacked me."

"Medical forensic evidence? How'd they get the goons?" Victor's eyes narrowed and he was very, very interested.

Doug rubbed at the stitches in his eyebrow again. "I managed to scratch each assailant quite hard — hard enough to break the skin — one with my right hand and one with my left, to keep the samples separate. I carefully protected the integrity of the evidence, although I'm afraid I had to be quite adamant at the hospital, where they kept insisting the dried blood was a biohazard. I believe they thought I was concussed and incoherent. People often seem to think that, even when I have not sustained a head injury…"

Doug looked distracted. Victor waited impatiently for him to gather his thoughts. "But in the end, Dr. Greenland…" And even though Victor was nodding his comprehension, Doug elaborated. "That's Toronto's head coroner. Dr. Greenland was able to take fingernail scrapings, and, using sophisticated DNA sampling, identified beyond a shadow of a doubt the two men who had attacked me."

"Coroner? Why the coroner? You certainly don't look dead to me." He reached over and placed the flat of his hand over Doug's heart. Doug's hand ghosted up over Victor's, then dropped to his lap. Victor withdrew his hand when Doug appeared to be getting antsy, and collided with Doug's arm on its way toward his eyebrow again.

"A medical examiner doesn't just work with dead bodies, Victor. In this instance, she was the one with the experience and equipment necessary for this sort of work. Dr. Greenland said herself, however, that it had been a long time since she'd worked on a live person. But she was able to gather the necessary samples, and, in short order, the two miscreants were brought up on charges of assault on an officer of the court."

Victor fisted the air in triumph. "That must have felt good, putting those jokers away for a long, long time. What a way to get a manicure, though."

Doug flushed and smiled, rolling and unrolling the edge of the tablecloth. KiKi refilled their duck of tea. "I must confess there was indeed some satisfaction in their rapid arrest and detainment. The trial, however, won't be for some time yet. As you are no doubt aware, the courts have a heavy docket, and —"

"Don't I fucking know it!" Victor interjected.

Doug didn't shudder this time, although something about his expression reminded Victor of a Sunday school teacher he'd once had. "I read the papers. I read the papers. You want dessert or coffee or something? Nah. Let's get going. I'm stuffed. Done like dinner," Victor announced, settling back and patting his own formerly flat stomach.

KiKi sauntered over, spanking the bill down in a sticky pool of nuk-naan sauce. Victor made a token protest and polite pretence of reaching for his wallet. Doug reminded him of their arrangement and insisted on paying. He extracted an appropriate amount of cash from his billfold, and placed it in KiKi's hand.

Victor rather liked the feeling of being treated to a meal. Too often, it seemed, he was the one who got stuck with the tab. He'd really have to start dating a better class of guy. He grinned and slapped Doug on the shoulder warmly as both men slid from the booth. "Thanks for dinner, Dougie ol' buddy."

An old-fashioned doorbell jangled annoyingly as they exited the restaurant. The early dusk surprised Victor; he hadn't been aware of time passing. He shoved a toothpick in his mouth, considering briefly how poorly mint-flavoured wood meshed with peanut sauce. They sauntered back up Isabella Street to Victor's car, the silence now companionable rather than awkward.

Half a block later, Victor asked, "So. What took you from the Great White North to Toronto? Business or pleasure?"

"Neither. Both." Victor was about to swat away the thumb at eyebrow again when Doug thwarted him by tugging his earlobe instead. "I'm not sure quite how to answer that question."

"Just tell me in your own words, Doug."

"My dad was killed."

"What do you mean, your dad w.. illed? Somebody murdered your father?" Victor's voice was harsh with his anger, indignation, sympathy, outrage.

"Yes, regrettably. And it turned out to be one of his best friends. It broke my heart. I had thought of him as a member of the family."

"So how'd you catch the guy?"

Doug looked a bit dismayed; Victor could have kicked himself for how insensitive he'd just sounded, but Doug ploughed on before Victor could make things worse.

"My father was shot while investigating some irregularities at a dam site in Northern Ontario. Around Latchford, actually. He was a Mountie."

Victor nodded.

"When I was contacted about his death, I volunteered to assist in the investigation to the best of my abilities. The RCMP tried to discourage me, but as I was a civilian, they had no actual authority over how I spent my time. I used my accounting training to follow the audit trail and managed to track the killers to Toronto and a group of funeral directors who'd been hunting up in the Canadian north."

"Your father was killed by funeral directors?" As if Victor hadn't hated funerals enough before hearing Doug's tale of woe.

"No. By a hired assassin posing as a funeral director. I tracked them to Toronto, and there worked with a detective from the Toronto PD — that's Police Department, Victor —"

"I know that, Doug."

"— to eventually apprehend the hired killer. We were then able to trace the original contract back to the man I had called Uncle."

"And that's when you decided to go into forensic accounting instead of just the regular numbers kind, right?"

Again Doug seemed stunned by Victor's grasp of the situation. "Yes. That's very perceptive of you. The RCMP was so impressed with my work that they gave me my first freelance contract."

Ah, thought Victor. That explained the faded crest on the shitty sweats Doug had worn for his workout.

Having long since reached the car, they finished their conversation with Victor perched on the trunk. Doug stood at an approximation of parade rest while finishing his story, gesticulating gracefully with his right hand while his left rested on his hip.

"I'm sorry about your dad, Doug. It must have been tough on you."

Doug studied the ground, white running shoes contrasting starkly with the rutted dirt. "It was. Especially since I'd lost my mother very young."

"Which is why you spent so much time with your grandparents," Victor filled in.

"Yes. Now they're gone. So Dad's pretty much the only family I have." Victor sympathized with Doug's continued use of the present tense. Takes a while to get used to loss, to putting *ex* in front of *wife*.

"Although…" Doug carried on, with furtive looks at the ramshackle buildings, virtually whispering, "I've heard I have a half-sister somewhere in the North."

Interesting as this True Confessions tangent might be, Victor wanted closure on the how-I-came-to-Toronto story and then to go home with Doug. And not necessarily in that order. The talk of long-ago transgressions that weren't actually his own could wait for another time. "Toronto, Doug. Do you like it here?"

"I don't mean to insult your home, Victor, but I find Toronto a challenging city to live in. I'm rather, well, lonely, I suppose you could say, despite the close personal friendship I formed with the detective who'd been in charge of my father's case."

Victor nodded. He'd had his own share of close personal friendships, if that's what the kids were calling it these days. "So you made this…friend here in Toronto, but you find it lonely anyway. Did you and he have a fight?"

"Not at all. My friend was transferred elsewhere — an assignment that he felt he had to take."

"So, you don't keep up with him? Not even by phone?"

Doug looked around suspiciously. Victor wondered what the hell he was looking for because they were very much alone back here behind these old buildings slated for demolition.

Apparently satisfied, Doug whispered, "He's undercover. He can't call."

Uh, oh, Victor thought. What a crappy way to dump your boyfriend. Not that he'd always been as honest as he should have been with his ex-lovers. He nodded again, starting to feel like one of those annoying drinking birds. He settled himself back against the windshield, the rear wiper digging into the small of his back a little, waiting to see just what Doug would say next. He craned his neck to get a better look, but Doug just moved away. Couldn't see very well in the twilight anyway.

"I was never able to reach him after that. I even tried calling some people I'd met at the police station, but they were equally cryptic. I found it difficult to get a straight answer."

"Hmmm. Well, there you go." Victor responded with some acknowledging nonsense. First he couldn't get the guy to open up, now he couldn't get him to shut up. Victor was starting to lose interest in the conversation portion of the evening. Still, if he offended the guy, there wouldn't be any other kind of portion to the evening.

Doug toyed with a bit of lint on his jeans. Victor thought he looked sad. "I still miss him, though. I haven't managed to make another friend like him since then." He stared moodily into the distance.

"Cheer up, buddy. You got me now, don't you? Your brand new best friend." Victor's beamed a brilliant smile in Doug's direction.

"Well, I, uh…"

Victor slid down and off the trunk. Two long strides and he paused at the driver's side, looking back. "Where can I drop you? Where'd you park?" He gestured back toward the gym with the damp toothpick, waving it like a tiny conductor's baton.

"Oh. I'm afraid I don't own a car. I took public transit from home. It's no trouble for me to walk. It's just a few blocks. Thank you very much for the kind offer, though."

"I got to drive myself home anyway. Where'd you say you lived?" In actuality, Victor had memorized Doug's vitals from the gym paperwork. Unfortunately, Toronto was a vast and sprawling city and Victor had never heard of the street on which Doug lived.

"I have an apartment in the Yonge and Eglinton area. It's just a few kilometers north of here. About a forty-five-minute walk, I'd estimate."

A forty-five minutes walk! Nobody walked like that. "C'mon, then. I gotta go right by there," Victor lied. "Besides, I'm holding your gym stuff hostage."

Grinning, he unlocked the driver's side door, swung in and over to let Doug in; the classic automobile well predated automatic locks. A long moment passed as Doug hovered uncertainly at the rear of the car, then, left without option, climbed into the passenger seat.

Victor bumped out of the makeshift parking lot driving far too quickly for the uneven ground. Doug shifted apprehensively, clearly questioning the wisdom of accepting Victor's offer of a ride. Realizing this, Victor drove more sedately up Yonge Street; the forty-five-minute walk covered by car in less than ten.

Victor lived in a funky old apartment building on Queen Street East, which was, in fact, nowhere near Yonge and Eglinton. But it wasn't that far out of his way. Especially since it seemed like it was going to be worth his while. He stole a sidelong glance at his passenger. *Very* worth his while. He licked his lips, his mind straying to other things that also involved tongues.

As they crossed St. Clair Avenue — about halfway to Doug's apartment — Victor figured it was high time for a little clarity. He searched for just the right words to ask, finally settling on, "I like to drive stick, Doug. How 'bout you?" Good. Good. Subtle, but not too subtle.

A short but informative lecture on the relative merits of automatic versus manual transmissions shed little definitive light on Doug's sexual orientation. It did, however, eat up the remainder of the drive to Doug's apartment. Still, all the clues added up, didn't they? And Victor was good at piecing clues together.

Having been given plenty of advance notice by his navigator, Victor turned onto a minor residential street. A couple more turns and he pulled up as directed in front of a low-rise apartment building whose architecture spoke of the '20s or '30s. It looked in okay shape to Victor, and he said so.

"It's more than adequate for my needs." Doug scrutinized his own building as if seeing it anew. "If you'd kindly assist me in retrieving my things from your trunk, I won't take up any more of your time this evening."

No more futzing around; time to shit or get off the pot, fish or cut bait, get down to business, stake the claim, can't get down if you don't get up, just do it! Enough already with the pep talk! Victor shut the car off, leaving the keys dangling from the ignition.

Nerves steeled for rejection, Victor slid over a bit, glad of the bench seats of the loaner car. "You in a hurry there, Doug?"

Doug whipped his head around and Victor closed the distance between them smoothly, managing to bring his lips down over Doug's with delightful precision: no skating off onto cheeks or inept clinking of teeth, despite the awkward position. Doug's gorgeous mouth opened under Victor's for a moment, then Doug pulled away quickly, smacking his skull resoundingly on the window glass, mouth still open, but in astonishment rather than welcome.

"I…I don't…I've never…Well…I don't kiss men," he finally choked out.

Victor puzzled a moment. "Okay. I get you. You don't kiss men. You're one of those…" He rolled his eyes. In his opinion, those bisexual men who fucked both genders but kissed only women needed professional help. Just deal. Wasn't the idea to make the most of each experience? He certainly intended to. "I am all over that."

Despite the early-evening shadows, Victor could clearly see the look of relief wash over Doug's face. "Thank you for understanding, Victor. I —" Victor drew his right hand up Doug's thigh, coming to rest on his crotch. Still watching Doug's face for clues, Victor expected, hoped even, to see pleasure, desire, happiness, horniness, but saw grim determination instead. Doug's seized Victor's deftly massaging hand, forcing it back down his leg, pinning it against the warm denim.

Huh? "You said no kissing, buddy, so I went with no kissing. You want to tell me what you like? I'm kind of in the dark here."

Doug reached toward his eyebrow with his free hand, but lowered it again before it reached its destination. "Women, Victor. I'm sorry, but I like women." He inhaled deeply, somehow sadly, meeting Victor's eyes, which were narrowed with scepticism. Victor glanced pointedly to where Doug's hand still secured Victor's to his thigh like a butterfly pinned to a cork. Following his gaze, Doug snatched away his hand. "I'm just…sorry."

Reluctantly, Victor reclaimed his hand, grasping the steering wheel like a life preserver. This guy was rocking his world and not in a good way. "No, Doug. I'm sorry. I must have read your signals wrong. I thought you were coming on to me tonight. You know, we just met, you asked me out, picked up the check, let me take you home."

Where was the flaw in his reasoning? He was good at going on instinct. He'd built his career on it. He felt in his gut that Doug found him attractive. But no means no, right? He should have known.

Doug's apology had taken on a life of its own. "I'm terribly sorry if I gave you the wrong impression. I did wish to compensate you for your time by taking you to dinner. And, to be totally honest, I did have an ulterior motive: a hidden agenda, as they say."

Victor waited for him to finish. Doug made another abortive attempt to scratch his eyebrow.

Doug seemed to be having difficulty with this part. "I, ah, well, I enjoyed the time we spent together, and I, um, don't have many friends, and I rather wanted you to have dinner with me." Doug appeared to be working this out as he went along. "So it's no wonder you arrived at the wrong conclusion. It's entirely my fault for giving you the incorrect impression. I really must apologize, Victor."

"No. Doug. It's not you. I'm just an aggressive son of a bitch. I had no right. And then I —" Victor flopped back in his seat. "I suck. I just...suck."

"Is that another offer, Victor? Because I'm afraid I must decline that as well, although no doubt you are very good at it."

What the fuck? Oh, shit. "No. No. I didn't mean that. I'm done coming on to you. I get it. I get it. I meant I suck. I'm an asshole. A jerk. It's no biggie." Jesus. What word didn't have homoerotic connotations? "An idiot. I didn't mean — I wasn't referring to — Oh, shit. I'm really sorry."

The car windows were milky with fog, not from heavy breathing, but from the blushing heat pouring off both men.

"Oh, well, then. I'm afraid I must apologize then. I assumed —"

"I'll get your stuff from the trunk." Doug looked grateful for the interruption and the chance of escape.

A few more apologies were exchanged; there was another awkward moment when Doug accidentally covered Victor's fingers with his own as he retrieved his gym bag. Then Doug was heading up the walk.

Climbing back into the driver's seat, Victor turned the key in the ignition.

The radio instantly began crooning about the pain of love lost.

"Shut the fuck up!" Victor savagely spun the old radio dial.

Now the lyrics extolled the virtue of being in the arms of your loved one.

Click! The loaner T-bird slipped through the night like a ghost. Victor wondered how hard it would be to replace the broken radio knob.

The following day Victor made it all the way through his workout and his shift before he finally succumbed to the compulsive pressure of his nerves. In his best casual stroll, he approached the gym manger, Phil Martini, at the front desk.

Phil sported a Day-Glo designer tracksuit, which, coupled with the flashy jewelry and shiny bald head, was nearly blinding. He clashed badly with his assistant Nelly's pale pink leotard, nails, lip gloss and sweatband. She snapped her gum energetically as she handed out towels next to him.

"So, um. Phil?" *Off to a good start, Brighton*, Victor chided himself.

The quintessential salesman, Phil immediately glanced up, sincerely meeting Victor's eyes and flashing him a peroxide-whitened smile — for the half second it took him to realize it was only one of his staff and not a potential new sale. "Yeah?" He returned to his paperwork, adding up his commissions for the week, no doubt. Which gave Victor an idea how to extract the information he wanted, subtly.

"How you doing, Phil? Raking in the dough?" Victor flipped his towel over one shoulder as he cut through the small break in the long, blue laminate counter, moving to peer over Phil's shoulder.

"I'm onto you, Brighton. No, I don't lend money and no, I can't influence the boss lady to give you a raise." He didn't look up. "Besides, I'm not doing all that well this week." But then, Phil never felt he did well enough in any given week.

"Ah. Okay, then." Victor thought he did crestfallen rather well. "But you got at least one commission for that guy yesterday."

"Oh, him. Yeah. He called earlier."

Oh, shit! Panic time. What if he'd told them Victor had hit on him? What if he brought up the steroid convo? What if he cancelled his membership? What if he sued? Shit. Shit. Shit! Victor should never have tried mixing business with pleasure. He knew that. Boy, did he know that.

Asking Phil what the guy had wanted taxed every bit of guile Victor possessed.

"Dunno. Didn't take the call. Nelly did."

Victor waited agonizing minutes for Nelly to finish with a customer who really just wanted to talk about her own progress: how much weight she'd lost, how much tone she'd gained, how many times she'd been asked out. Finally, trying to make his interruption sound terribly official, he cut into a story in which lettuce featured largely. The self-absorbed Amazon wandered away, and Victor, lowering his voice in hopes that Phil wouldn't hear, said, "You took a call today."

"I take calls every day, Victor. All day. Every day, all day. Hey, hey. That reminds me of —"

Victor cut in abruptly this time. "It was from a guy who started here yesterday. Doug Newkirk. Ring any bells?"

Sighing audibly, Nelly gazed off at the glass brick wall surrounding the aerobics room. "Oh, yeah. Doug."

"Nelly. What did he want? What'd he say?"

"Oh. Just confirmed his four thirty training session with you Friday, Victor. Did you know he was an accountant?" Her eyes sparkled as if *accountant* meant *Prince Charming* on Planet Nelly.

"He asked for me? By name?"

"Yes, Victor." She squinted at him for a minute. "He specifically asked for you. Said if you weren't available then, he'd come whenever you were free." She scrunched her eyes and shook her head in an expression of disbelief. Victor was inclined to agree.

But incredulity was overwhelmed by joy. He almost did a little dance right there in the front office area, singing inwardly:

I'm not going to get sued. I'm not going to get my cute li'l ass canned. He slung his arm around Nelly and kissed her on the cheek.

"Okay. Okay. What was that for?" She brushed her hand over her cheek, not as if wiping it away, more just to…savor the experience. Victor resolved to show Nelly his appreciation more often; she looked so happy. "Hey, Victor," she called after him. "How come all the good ones are taken or gay?" She was pretty swift on the uptake, after all.

He mimed a limp wrist in her direction and headed toward the stairs. Although he was more on the bi side — hell, he'd been married for years — he'd rebuffed her advances early on by assuring her he was completely, 100% gay: a veritable six on the Kinsey scale. She'd backed off and been a good friend after that, almost like the sister he'd never had. Nor really wanted, come to think of it.

"Hey, Victor." He turned back toward the desk as Phil called after him. "Did you forget? You're supposed to see Ms. Amorotique now." To Victor's puzzled expression, Phil added, "You know? The new owner?" Victor had indeed forgotten — shit. He hadn't forgotten who Veronica Amorotique was, just that he had an appointment with her. "She's just in with someone. Go get changed and she'll probably be ready by then."

"You…that is, Phil said you wanted to see me?"

Intended as a statement, it came out in a quizzical tone as Victor, now changed into faded blue jeans and a navy T-shirt, hovered in the doorway of the gym owner's office. By far the nicest room in the building, it featured postmodern blond wood furniture and chrome high-tech accents. It had recently been renovated, and there were still a few things the contractors had yet to finish. The bare walls and dangling wires made an interesting contrast with the expensive designer furnishings. Victor figured she used cheap and therefore slow contractors as a way to save money. The bare wires were a hazard, though, and most certainly not up to code.

"Hello, Victor." She glanced up at him from behind the executive desk that was more like a big pine table. It had no modesty panel at the front, and Victor found himself somewhat smitten with her stockinged feet. They were incredibly sensual, with tasteful plum nail polish and pricey seamless hose. The spike-heeled pumps rested in a sexy little heap to one side. He knew all about hose and pumps and polish from his years married to Yolanda. And from his car, of course.

"Or do you prefer *Vic?*" She rubbed her feet together lovingly, silkily, and he felt a frisson of excitement travel down his spine. He hadn't been with a woman since Yolanda, having slipped into the habit of men when they split up — no complications for this newly bachelorized guy. Nice to have options.

"Victor? Victor!" He realized he was staring and quickly shifted his glance from sexy bare feet to gorgeous eyes, hair, face…and was amazed to see her own eyes staring at him hungrily. Her gaze pointedly ran up and down his body, pausing a beat at crotch, then lips, before returning to eyes. "I wanted to have a little meeting with you to discuss your progress with the organization." Her voice trailed off as she stared hard into his eyes. "But I can't get away from the paperwork at the moment." She gestured vaguely toward her desk, clear but for a single, short stack of membership forms. She cleared her throat. "I don't like to leave my employees dangling. Do you think you could come back in an hour or so and maybe we could do this over dinner instead?" She looked all wistful and pretty.

Eventually "sure" emerged from the mesmerized Victor.

"Eight-ish?" she said brightly, dismissively, turning back to her paperwork. Victor left feeling both turned on and, for some reason, slightly used. They were not, however, mutually exclusive events for a man formerly married to Yolanda Summerwood-Brighton.

✕ ✕ ✕

"That certainly is an interesting vehicle, Victor. It's very…shiny."

"Yeah. Thanks." He handed her out and slammed the passenger door behind her. "I just got it detailed." He eyed his newly returned GTO with pride. Veronica spared it hardly a glance as she headed toward her building, high heels clicking on the pavement.

"Thank you for seeing me up to my condo." Victor rubbernecked, taking in the forty-five stories of green glass. Good thing he didn't have a thing about heights. "I never feel safe in a big city. I'm from Nova Scotia originally."

"I'd think you'd feel plenty safe here, Veronica, what with the twenty-four-hour security and the surveillance cameras and the concierge guy and all." He looked around the spacious mirrored lobby. "This is real nice. The front entrance alone is bigger than my entire apartment. Better decorated, too." Veronica gave him a slightly displeased look. Oops. Better to let her figure out the crappy existence that was his life on her own — no need to go giving her the guided tour.

They entered the chrome-and-mirror elevator to the strains of somebody and his orchestra butchering '80s techno-pop. "I got better tunes, though." He grinned, winked, and drummed a decent beat on the handrail framing the elevator.

Veronica favored him with a brief smile in return as she dug through her purse, eventually pulling out keys triumphantly. Victor had a brief vision of Bullwinkle J. Moose: *Watch me pull a rabbit outta my hat.* Disaster had struck the moose every Saturday; Victor could so relate. Okay. Rejection time, here it comes. It's not too late to still hit a nightclub for a little dance floor action.

He trailed along behind his boss as she headed down the hall at a brisk pace, keys in hand. "Well, Victor. I had an enjoyable evening. It was a pleasant way to tell you how pleased I am with your work at my gym. And you clean up very nicely, I might add." She ran a possessive gaze down his body. In the time between their quickie interview and their subsequent dinner, Victor had charged home, shaved, and changed into fairly new black jeans, a gray Henley and stylish gray jacket. Silently, he blessed his friend Johnnie, who worked retail and had forced him to buy the jacket during a post-Yolanda shopping excursion. It was supposed to cheer Victor up, and had, to some extent, until his MasterCard bill came in.

"Thank you. I appreciate the feedback. I'm glad you're, um, pleased with my performance. Um. Good night." He turned to leave her at her open door.

"What? You're not coming in?" She tossed her long dark curls over one shoulder and frowned at him expectantly.

Victor turned back around, quickly retracing his steps. "Didn't realize I'd been invited." He tried to modulate the huge grin into something...cooler. And failed.

"Of course you're invited in. Have a seat." She indicated the couch by the long window with the lake view. Victor wondered if the apartment smelled of fish in the summer. "Can I get you something to drink?" She removed her silk jacket and stepped out of her spiky shoes, padding over to the bar near the floor-to-ceiling windows.

"Sure. Beer's fine. Oh. Okay. White wine's fine, too." He reached for the bottle she held in one hand so she could deal with the two crystal glasses in the other. "Nice digs you got here. Guess the gym business pays pretty well, eh?"

"I do all right, thank you." Victor read not modesty in her voice, but disinterest — probably in his opinion altogether, he mused, wondering why he was here if she didn't much care for him. Talk about your mixed signals. "And thank you for dinner, by the way. You really should have let me get it. After all, I can write it off as a business expense... I think." She trailed off.

She poured equal amounts of the yellow liquid into each glass. Victor always thought white wine looked uncomfortably like piss — he much preferred beer, which also, come to think of it... He shied away from any further urine comparisons.

"You could ask that new guy who just signed up this week — he's an accountant," Victor offered, the new guy being very much on his mind after last night.

"Hmmm. That's an idea." She actually looked at him as she handed him his glass. "I could use a good bookkeeper."

Seating herself on the sofa close to him, Veronica pulled her bare feet up under her, causing her short skirt to ride high on her thighs. "Victor. I wanted to get you out of the gym to talk about something else." She turned to face him, bracing an elbow on the sofa back and resting her head on one hand. Her long spiral curls streamed down her face and arm like syrup. "There's a lot of talk going round the gym about steroid use. I thought maybe, being on the floor and all, you might be able to tell me something about it."

Caught mid sip, Victor choked on his wine. Shit. Shit. Shit. Somebody'd told her about his comments to Doug yesterday. She's going to give me grief. She's going to can my ass. She's waiting for an answer.

"Well, um..." Great start, Victor. He stalled for time while he formed an answer. He needed to know why she was asking this particular question, where she was going with this. "I have heard a few things, not specific to your gym of course, but I've been around, you know, worked at more than one gym."

"Yes. I read your résumé. I review all potential employees before I permit Phil to hire them. Interesting that every health club you've ever worked for is now out of business." She eyed him suspiciously.

"Well, you know the gym business, here today, and —" He realized how badly this sentence would go over with his current employer, "So many of the other clubs are mismanaged. Every gym rat thinks they can run a club."

"Luckily I have the acumen to run a successful business." She flipped her curls over one shoulder, "But I want to know about you and steroids. Have you ever been approached to buy any? Have you ever used them?"

She glanced at his wiry frame. Not likely; he certainly didn't have the boggy swamp look that most of the juicers got — or the pizza back, or the bitch tits, thank God. He shuddered to think about some of the dreadful cases of acne he'd seen across the backs and shoulders of some of the guys — and gals — at the gym. Although the enlarged nipples on some of the guys could be kind of interesting. And he'd heard that testosterone in women could cause enlargement of the...

"Have you ever thought about selling them?" All innocent doe eyes, Veronica met and held his gaze. "I can understand the temptation of that kind of cash."

Her eyes left his and swept around the grand apartment.

"I, um, wouldn't mind making some extra cash from time to time." His breathing became harsh, his heart sped up — he always got excited at times like these.

"Well, Victor." She trailed her fingers over the back of his bare forearm. "If you were to hear about anyone buying or wanting to buy steroids or human growth hormone, you make sure you come and tell me." Her hand, cool and a bit clammy, came to rest on his wrist.

"Yeah. Well. You want to know something about this steroid business, Ronnie? Veronica, I mean." He corrected himself quickly at her look of displeasure. "I could keep an ear to the ground for you." He restrained his urge to run a conspiratorial thumb down his nose. After yesterday, that felt like an intimacy shared by Doug and him since they'd used it during yesterday's steroid discussion.

"Do that for me, would you, please, Victor? I want to know everything you hear about steroids in my gym."

"Okay, it's a plan." He placed his mostly empty wine glass on the table and rose to leave. She tightened her grip on his wrist and half pulled him towards her, eyeing him like a fine leather handbag. On sale. She leaned in and quickly covered his lips with her own — a repeat of his recent assault on Doug, only the shoe was on the other foot, or off the other foot, so to speak. He hesitated a moment, then pulled away, panting just a little.

"Oh, God, Veronica. I'm so sorry. I've given you the wrong signals here. I thought you knew." He trailed off.

"Knew what, Victor? Knew what?" Her confusion gave way to obvious anger in those few words.

Victor took her hand in both of his and searched her face for understanding. "I'm gay, Veronica. I thought you knew. I thought everybody knew."

Oddly, not understanding but impatience was reflected in her lovely features. "Well, I had actually heard that, but I wasn't sure it was true. You're such a…masculine man, Victor." She pulled her hand free and caressed his shoulder.

"Yeah. Well, I'm told I do butch very well." He pulled back a little from her touch. Her makeup-clogged pores were visible as she brought her face closer still, lips just centimeters from his.

"But your résumé says you were married. For years and years."

"And now I'm not." That wasn't a road he wanted to go down. With her. With anyone. Ever.

"That means you're bisexual, then."

"Yeah. Sure. Bisexual. I like men *and* boys."

Ignoring his attempt at humor and distance, Veronica advanced on him like a snake on a bird. "Maybe you just haven't met the right woman yet," she purred, moving her hand to the back of his neck and catching at the fine, light hairs there, a gesture of both caress and capture.

Oh, shit! Victor thought. She's one of those! Women who get off on trying to convert gay men. Mind whirling too much for him to concoct a suitable lie, he fell back on the truth. "Actually, I did meet the right woman, but she divorced me."

Instead of getting the point, Veronica seemed to think he was making hers for her. "Oh, poor baby. She hurt poor li'l you and now you've given up on women for good."

Don't women get that baby talk is not a turn-on for men? Victor flinched as she caressed his cheek. "Why don't you just let Veronica take care of you for a while?" she continued.

He drew back even further, scrambling his way backward along the couch. She followed him, pressing her heaving bosom against his quaking chest.

"Don't you find me attractive?" Not a trace of insecurity in her tone, she shook back her glorious mane of hair and waited for him to flatter her.

He captured her questing hand and pulled it above his waist. She seemed to think this was progress and leaned in for another attempt at a kiss.

"Ronnie!" he barked out, finally getting her attention with the hated diminutive. "Veronica. I do. I do find you attractive. I'd have to be dead not to." She received this like a monarch accepting a royal tithing. Victor hurried on. "I'm involved with somebody. I wouldn't…couldn't do this to him. Much as I'm tempted. Very tempted." He placed a kiss on her open palm, clutching it to his chest to prevent any further groping. He hadn't wanted to create a web of lies — they were too difficult to keep track of. Oh, what a tangled web and all that jazz. And he was tempted; Veronica was indeed a strikingly beautiful woman, but being with her would be a bad idea in general, and being with another woman still felt like cheating on Yolanda.

He was pretty sure Veronica was finally getting the message, but after last night's lesson in the suicidal practice of mixing business with pleasure, he wanted to be really sure. "Besides, don't you think it's generally a bad idea to sleep with the boss?" He tried a grin, but she wasn't ready for that yet.

Surprising him with her strength, she snatched back her hand, furious. "You think sleeping with the boss is a bad idea, just wait till you see what a bad idea *not* sleeping with the boss is!" Her voice was low and threatening. Maybe he should have just slept with her. Too late now. Boy, was she pissed. Hell hath no fury, as they say.

"I think I'd better go now" and "Get out!" tumbled over one another, the former spoken apologetically, the latter shrieked in rage.

Victor closed the door gently behind him, careful not to let it slam. The noise of a blunt object hitting the inside — a shoe maybe — followed closely on the snick of the lock.

Uh, oh. I think I'm in for some trouble. Wonder if this'll affect my performance review? The disastrous events of the last two evenings tangled and tangoed in Victor's troubled thoughts as he drove home in his shiny car, radio safely off.

LOVE IS A MANY-GENDERED THING

Victor checked his schedule anxiously first thing Friday morning before beginning his own workout. His hands were damp as he held the aging and dog-eared clipboard in a white-knuckled grasp. *Doug Newkirk: Personal Training, 4:30PM* jumped off the page as if embossed in scarlet. His stomach fluttered with relief — no lawsuit — then fluttered again as he thought of seeing Doug, of a possible…confrontation at worst, uncomfortable silence at best. "God, I suck!" flashed across his memory, and he blushed and grinned simultaneously. "Yeah. I do," he said aloud, to no one in particular. "And I've never had any complaints."

He grabbed a towel from the pile Nelly was industriously folding, blew her a kiss in response to her annoyed "Hey! Those are for members only!" and headed for the aerobics area, empty at this hour, to do a little stretching and warm-up before heading up for his own workout.

Victor's confidence faded in and out during his shift, replaced by apprehension and anticipation in just about equal measures. It was a huge relief when Doug showed up fifteen minutes early, thereby cutting short Victor's anxiety cycle before he actually did damage to himself or any of the gym's other clients.

"Hi, Victor." Doug's voice seemed calm, but when Victor peered closely, he thought he detected a bit of tension beneath the glossy exterior.

Oh, shit. I'm staring at the poor guy, Victor realized when Doug coughed politely and raised one eyebrow in a Spock-like motion.

"Oh. Yeah. Um." Off to a slow start, he then burst into a verbal barrage. "Today we'll do a full circuit workout, mainly on the machines, then we'll talk about some aerobic exercise. Got to get you started off right." Nervousness fading a little, he led

Doug to a machine that worked chest and showed him how to set the weights, marking them on the little pre-printed card all the newbies were given.

The threat of actual conversation hung heavily between them. Victor limited any exchanges to the strictly practical descriptions of equipment, muscles and form. Doug seemed to have little or no background in modern fitness beliefs and practices, and Victor found himself backing up his statements again and again, explaining terminology and popular health philosophies as he went along. Doug had a vast general knowledge, including musculature and physiology, obtained largely through reading, he explained. He seemed lost, though, when he attempted to apply this learning to the various fitness "truths" Victor was laying out for him.

"Ah. I wasn't aware that muscle could turn into fat, Victor. It just doesn't seem biologically possible."

"Well, that's what I've always heard. Maybe the molecules, I don't know, morph or something. Anyway, it's not the literal meaning; it's the motivational thought that counts. You know, sort of metashitical. Now quit stalling and do another set."

Partway through the workout Doug became winded and sweaty, straining to complete the exercises Victor had set for him, even with relatively light weight. Conversation fizzled out altogether as Doug used the brief periods between sets to recuperate for the next one.

Doug didn't whine, nor utter a word of complaint, though. He was no wimp; Victor had to give him that.

"We're almost done, Doug. You want to take a little rest here?"

That Doug limited himself to a grateful nod was more telling than any heartfelt words. He sat heavily on a nearby workout bench that made little farting noises as the air escaped through the cheap red vinyl. He looked vaguely embarrassed, but Victor just waved it away, and Doug let it go. Victor brought one foot up to rest on the bench next to Doug and leaned both arms on his raised knee. He kept a watchful eye on his client to make sure he didn't expire right there on the bench.

Eventually Doug regained his breath enough to ask Victor about his own workout curriculum.

"Well, I've been at this a while — since high school," he elaborated at Doug's quizzical look. "Started with gym class, wrestling, boxing, hockey…"

Doug's eye's lit up at the mention of hockey. "I played a lot of hockey myself growing up in the North — pond hockey mostly. We didn't have proper rinks in most of the towns where I lived." He drew in a deep breath, almost gasping. "I was certainly in better shape then. I can't believe how soft I've let myself get. Even Jack has told me so. Repeatedly."

"Right. So I do a triple-split workout, which is different from the full-circuit program I've got you on." Like most fitness types, Victor really liked to talk about himself — his workouts, his progress, his weight and his weights. He wondered who Jack was, and thought he might remember to ask some other time.

"How so?"

"You're new to this, so I'm not working you all that hard. That means your muscles don't need as long to recover. I've got you working out every other day. Me, I work my muscles that much harder so they need a longer rest period, so I work out three days on, one day off."

Doug leaned back slightly to look up at Victor. "I fail to see how working out six times a week allows your muscles more recovery time than working out three times a week."

"Hmm. I can see where you might find that counter…um, counterintuitive." Victor was pleased at having worked that into the conversation. Doug had a huge vocabulary and Victor was trying hard to keep up. Still, he knew more about fitness, local restaurants, and classic cars than Doug, so maybe he shouldn't be trying so hard. It's not like he was trying to get into the guy's good graces, or, say, pants, or anything. Not after last night.

Victor turned his mind back to the fitness lecture. "It's like this. You're new at this so everything you do is going to help. The program I've designed for you makes sure you hit every major muscle group a little every time you work out. Then you get one day off for your muscles to recuperate, right?"

At Doug's nod, he continued. "But I break my workout up so that it takes me three days to do my whole body." A small quiver of excitement tickled Victor's spine as Doug ran his eyes down then back up the body under discussion. He hoped Doug liked what he saw. "So day one is back and shoulders; day two, legs and triceps; day three, chest and bis…er, biceps. And I try and do some cardio every day, even the days off. That reminds me, we need to get you started on cardio. You said something about running the other day." He almost blushed at the mention of the other day.

"Yes. Actually, I started that night. I found I had" — Doug cracked his neck sharply to the right; Victor winced in sympathy at the painful-sounding popping — "some trouble sleeping, and so went for a short jog around eleven. I also ran the next day as well as yesterday, and found it a bit easier already."

Victor was impressed. He'd been right about this guy, although most people started out with enthusiasm; sooner or later, their interest waned, usually sooner.

"Don't overdo it, guy. You don't want to strain anything. Do you know what you're doing — like with form and running gear and shit?"

Doug seemed to have adjusted to Victor's continual use of profanity in his colorful speech, the flinching no longer evident. "I wasn't aware there was that much involved in running. I just went out in these shoes and ran."

"Jeez, Doug. You wouldn't set out to, um, snowshoe or something without the right gear, would you? Running's no different." He was mildly pleased he'd been able make his point in terms Doug could relate to from his upbringing in the far north.

"Well, when you put it that way, Victor. Perhaps you could advise me on some of the technicalities?"

"You mean like take you shopping? Yeah. I could do that." Victor heard the words come out of his mouth before he thought about them. His stomach performed another flip-flop as he realized how this might sound.

"Oh, that's kind of you, Victor. I'd certainly appreciate that, but I fear I've taken up too much of your personal time already. Perhaps I could pay you for your time — sort of a consultant fee." He gave Victor a small smile that was both warm and lopsided.

Victor couldn't believe his luck that this guy was so completely cool with the…misunderstanding of the other night. Instead, Doug was trying to pay him. Maybe he felt more in control if he paid Victor…paid him to what? For just his charming company? Right. Pull the other one. Victor decided to play this a bit and see where it went. He still had trouble believing Doug wasn't at all inclined that way. Even though he respected "no means no", he just thought he'd test the waters a wee bit.

Flirtatiously he asked, "How much were you thinking?" He stopped himself from adding "Sailor." Doug appeared to be an awfully literal kind of guy at times, and he didn't want a lecture on land versus sea career choices. In the background, the cut-rate sound system hissed out the new version of Lady Marmalade. *Great*, Victor thought: *my life has a soundtrack.*

Doug must have given his offer some prior thought, because, "Does $50 sound like enough to you?" came out without a lot of um-ing and ah-ing.

Victor made like he was thinking this over, then counteroffered: "Fifty bucks doesn't sound quite right to me. What with my skills and expertise, 'n' all. How's forty?"

Doug's eye grew wide, then narrowed quickly as he got it. "Thirty."

"Twenty."

"Ten."

Now I feel like a ten-buck fuck, Victor's inner bitch snapped. "Okay. I'll make a deal with you, then it's time to finish your workout and skedaddle. I'll take you shopping." He glanced at the clock, as if that would help him recall his prior commitments. "Not this weekend. The Saturday after, but you gotta buy me lunch first. Deal?" He didn't have much planned for this weekend; had to work Saturday and maybe a game on Sunday, but he didn't want to overwhelm the guy. Yolanda had made it abundantly clear to him that he could be hard to take in large doses.

"Deal." Victor grasped Doug's outstretched hand to shake on it, then used it to yank Doug to his feet and propel him to his last few sets.

Let's Do Lunge

The week passed swiftly. Victor had given Doug a training schedule that allowed for weekends off, but got the impression that Doug didn't have a heck of a lot else to fill his time.

Victor thought about his new sort-of-friend a bit over the weekend. He didn't know quite what to make of the whole thing, but thought he'd enjoy whatever came of it. He didn't have a whole hell of a lot to occupy his own time outside of work, so a new friend was always welcome. It wasn't like his own dance card was so terrifically full. He'd filled his time since Yolanda with casual flings and empty sex. He'd cut himself off from his former coworkers when he took the job at the gym. So the gym was good and a new friend was good; and since both involved Doug, therefore Doug was good. Victor found himself looking forward to Monday for the first time in his life.

Doug joined Victor punctually in the gym on each of their appointed training times: Monday, Wednesday, and Friday. It was too early to show much progress. At this point all Doug was getting for his trouble was sore muscles.

Friday found Doug grunting and struggling to move the inverted platform of the leg press machine up and down in a controlled manner. Sweat darkened the neck and underarms of his light blue T-shirt.

"Keep your knees slightly bent at all times, Doug." Victor crouched beside the machine, bringing himself down to eye level with his straining protégé. "If you hyperextend — that means lock your knees — you can do yourself damage."

Doug just nodded, tongue whipping out to lick away the sweat forming on his upper lip. He carefully finished the last extension of his third and final set, and flipped the support bars back into place. Victor started to remove the forty-five pound plate from the right side, expecting Doug to do the same on the left.

Doug, it seemed, was having a little trouble extracting himself from the piece of equipment that required him to sit at floor level with his back supported at a forty-five degree angle, and his legs spread almost straight above him. Under other circumstances, it would have been a very erotic position. Victor wondered who had the keys to lock up at night and then absolutely refused to wonder if all the dark watermarks on the carpet were sweat.

"Need a hand there, buddy?"

"Certainly not, thank you." The words were polite but spoken witheringly. "I assure you I am quite capable of getting up off the floor. A very dirty floor, I might add."

Without further comment, Victor walked round to the other side of the apparatus and removed the remaining plate. Doug looked like he might say something for a moment, then just nodded gratefully.

"It's been a long week, Doug. You can use a couple days off. Let the lactic acid that's built up in your muscles revert back into whatever it is it reverts back into. But you can't take more than the weekend off or it will never stop hurting. Gotta build up those inosine levels in your blood so you don't hurt after every workout."

Doug looked at him skeptically, raising one eyebrow. Victor wondered again just how accurate all his "fitness facts" were — after all, he'd just learned all this stuff from other boxers and muscleheads. Screw it. It's the end results that count. Once you've been working out regularly, you don't hurt nearly as much. End of story.

"Problem is, you don't hurt while you're working out, so you don't know to moderate your exercise. Then the next day you're dying of the pain, and the really tragic thing is you know no matter how much you hurt the day after your workout, it's going to hurt even more the next day."

"Then why am I working out every second day? Doesn't that mean you have me working out on exactly the days that it hurts the most?" Doug heaved himself out of the mass of iron, solder, and gray rust paint.

"Yeah. But it's all just temporary. Pretty soon you won't hurt so bad — it's called paying your dues. No pain, no gain. What doesn't kill you, makes you stronger, right? Now let's get outta here — if you can."

Victor slapped Doug soundly on his sweaty back and grabbed their towels from a nearby bench. He tossed Doug his and threw his own over his shoulder. "Let's get outta here. Call it an early night. You and me, we got us a big shoe shopping date tomorrow, remember?" He certainly hoped Doug remembered — he'd feel like a big goof if Doug cancelled on him now, after he'd brought it up like he didn't have anything better to do on his one Saturday off a month.

Doug wiped his shiny forehead with the towel, then grasped Victor's arm tightly as he headed toward the doorway, halting them both. "Just to prevent any further misunderstandings, Victor, it's not a date. Right?" His words were precise, and his eyes burned into Victor's.

Victor's eyes were on the hand that gripped his bicep just a little too tightly. He raised one eyebrow and smirked.

Doug released him hastily.

"Right. No problem. Definitely not a date. Got it. I got it." Babbling done, he headed to the front desk to finish some paperwork, taking his leave of Doug in the stairwell as he dragged himself toward the basement change room. Like clockwork, the junior gangbangers appeared on the stairs beneath them just as Victor was saying, "So I'll see you noon tomorrow at the Holy Grill in the Eaton Centre. Get us a table and I'll find you."

"Hey, look, guys. It's Ben," Levon called cheerfully. "Ben and Phil!"

Doug and Victor looked at the kid expectantly. Victor wondered who Ben and Phil were, since Phil Martini was off for the evening.

"Ben Dover and Philip McCrackie!" Levon howled with laughter, his homies collapsing in fits of un-banger-like snickering.

Victor rolled his eyes. Doug looked completely baffled.

Victor felt such a juvenile and ancient crack deserved a reply in kind: "Last time I heard that one, I laughed so hard I nearly fell off my dinosaur." He didn't care on his own account, but he bristled at the disparaging remarks. In his books, all prejudice sucked. Still, he reminded himself, he understood where Levon was coming from.

He gestured with his eyes that Doug should carry on down the stairs, running his thumb along his nose when Doug continued to look puzzled for another long moment of the gang-giggling soundtrack. He waited until Doug had turned the corner and Levon and crew were heading up to the third floor before he turned toward the front desk again. God, Doug was so clueless, so innocent. He thought about the beating Doug had taken before they'd even met and felt a sudden desire to protect his naïve friend. He smiled at the thought: Doug as friend. A bit premature yet, the guy was still offering to pay him for his company, but that was just part of the whole male bonding trip, wasn't it? Yeah. Doug as friend. He liked that, looked forward to their little shoe shopping expedition.

His final thought before turning his mind to paperwork was just how gay that sounded — straight men did not go shoe shopping together as a bondage, er, bonding activity. He wondered if the Leafs were playing.

He dropped off the dirty towel he'd purloined a week ago — staff were supposed to supply their own — and spent the next twenty minutes completing his small pile of paperwork with the minimum amount of effort, accuracy and detail required.

He stuck his time sheet into Phil's inbox and headed for the stairs.

"Hey, Victor!" Nelly grabbed him just as he was heading out. "Was that Doug I just saw with you?" Her gum snapped audibly as she fiddled with the scheduling books on the counter in front of her. "Veronica wants to talk to him."

"Nah. Some other guy. Doug won't be back till next week sometime."

"But the schedule says —"

"Have yourself a nice weekend, Nelly," echoed back up the stairs as Victor too, headed for the change room.

"She wants to see you, too, Victor," Nelly called down the stairs after him. "Now!"

He picked up his pace, charging for the locker room like the devil herself was after him. He so did not want to deal with the crazy boss lady's rejection issues, her gay-conversion issues, her steroid issues, or indeed any type of issues today. He didn't mind being the undercover guy at the gym, indeed spying for her fit in well with his own *modus operandi,* he just didn't have anything worthwhile to report…yet.

Victor tore through the department store at the north end of the mall. He was pissed at himself for hurrying, but he couldn't seem to relax. He'd deliberately slow down, stroll a few steps, then find himself rushing past the glitzy displays and provocative mannequins. He'd woken early this morning, then forced himself to take his time getting ready, hair spikes lined up like so many soldiers on parade. He'd left his apartment late, then driven like a maniac. It seemed he was powerless to be fashionably late for his rendezvous with Doug.

Noon-o-one. Right on time. Fuck. What if he got there before Doug? That would be, like, so uncool. "I'm meeting someone. I'll just take a quick look-see, 'kay?" He moved swiftly past the host or hostess; not looking at the person long enough to determine gender.

And, of course, there was good ol' Doug, sitting at a booth by the window, carefully measuring an exact teaspoon of sugar for his coffee. And Victor coming up on him suddenly, barking, "Hey, Doug!" caused him to drop spoon, sugar container, and sugar all over the table.

Victor couldn't help but chuckle. Pretty nervous for definitely-not-a-date. He slid into the booth across from Doug and watched with amusement while he carefully tidied up the spilled sugar. Seeking out and licking from his fingers every last grain. Victor found the pink flash of tongue on fingers simultaneously a turn-on and a gross-out; who knew how clean that tabletop was?

"I was here a little early, so I ordered coffee. I hope you don't mind."

"No problemo. I had a fair amount of caffeine before I left the house myself." Victor grabbed the menu and perused the contents. "I usually have the portobello 'shroom and goat's milk cheese sandwich here. What looks good to you?"

"Well, I was considering the specials which are —" Doug glanced up, staring directly over Victor's head, a look almost of alarm on his face.

Victor was just about to turn around when gentle, rather hairy arms wrapped themselves around his shoulders. "Well, I certainly know what looks good to me! And it's very *special*," came a familiar voice from above his head. Doug gazed worriedly at the new arrivals as Victor's old friend Johnnie slid his slender frame around Victor and into the seat next to him, barely loosening the wrestling hold. "You look great, hon," he told Victor, half-releasing him from the ongoing hug, leaving one arm across the back of the seat, "but I gotta say, *he* looks even better!" Johnnie practically leered at Doug, which made Victor feel a little embarrassed and little proprietary.

Johnnie's partner, Maurice, stood by their table, glaring at his now-seated companion. "What Johnnie actually means is, do you mind if we join you?" And did so at Doug's polite gesture toward the empty space beside him.

"Victor. It's so good to see you. Please introduce us to your pretty friend." Victor's new seatmate focused on Doug, resting his chin on both fists.

Victor cleared his throat several times. "Um. Johnnie Bauerman, Maurice Richards. This is Doug Newkirk. Doug, this is Johnnie," he patted the shoulder of the man on his left, "and Maurice." Hands were shaken, menus distributed, coffee almost knocked over, the waitress sent away for more drinks and another few minutes to decide.

Johnnie, his usual outgoing self, launched into a long story about a rude clerk, a lost sale and the beautiful new sweater that he'd purchased somewhere else at half the price. He whipped it out of its shopping bag with a flourish, draping it across one arm and up to his neck. "Notice the way it highlights my striking green eyes," he invited, batting his lashes.

"Colored contacts," Maurice muttered as he rescued the right sleeve from Victor's coffee cup, which, luckily, was empty at this point.

Victor hid a smirk behind his menu, just waiting for Johnnie to make some rebuttal involving his partner's ever-increasing forehead.

Instead, Doug asked questions and drew out the shopping tale. Fashionable Johnnie was in his glory, completely focused on the attractive man who seemed fascinated by his sale sweater saga. Johnnie ran a well-manicured hand over his shiny dark brown curls, unnecessary since they were as well ordered as Doug's own.

Maurice rolled his eyes and ordered for both when the waitress reappeared. Victor ordered his Portobello sandwich and Doug said he'd try one too.

"So, Victor." Apparently Johnnie had finished regaling Doug with stories of shopping triumphs and was now lasering his focus at Victor. "How long have you two been seeing each other? I hadn't heard anything through the grapevine and I'm deeply offended. I thought everyone knew all new information must go through my central gossip clearinghouse."

"We're not…We aren't…Doug's not…" Victor sputtered.

"This is only the second time we've been out socially, Johnnie," Doug elaborated. "We met recently when I joined the gym where Victor works."

"Where I work out." Victor's added swiftly. "Where I work out. That's where we met." He desperately tried to think of something to change the subject, then remembered that with Johnnie around he didn't have to.

"Only the second date. Oh, Maurice. Remember our second date?" Johnnie reached across the table to try and clasp his partner's hand. Maurice moved it deftly out of reach before Johnnie could strike.

"I most certainly do. You drank too much and spilled Remy Martin on my new jacket. You were lucky there was ever a third date." His warm smile belied the cranky words.

"No, Maury. *You* were lucky," Johnnie replied archly, then sat back and sighed. "Young love. It's…" He sat forward sharply, eyes glittering like a raven's. "Can I tell Yolanda? Please? Please? I'm such a yenta," he explained to Doug. "I can't help it. It's in the blood."

"No! No telling Yolanda. There's nothing to tell. We're just friends." Victor found two disbelieving expressions aimed his way. "Guys, Doug's straight."

Johnnie looked shocked, gaze shooting from Victor to Doug and back, finally gasping in disbelief: "Oh, Victor, say it ain't so!" Miming horror at Victor's nod, he cried in mock anguish, "Why is it all the good ones are either taken or straight?"

Maurice studied Doug curiously.

Doug looked like he would have bolted from the restaurant if one hundred and eighty pounds of Maurice Richards hadn't been effectively pinning him in his seat. In rapid succession, he picked up knife, then fork, dropped them, polished them, lined them up. The others watched as if he were the afternoon's entertainment, until… "Ah. Our food has arrived." Doug made himself of such help to the waitress that she finally left in a huff.

"Straight, eh? You married?" Johnnie eyed him suspiciously, ignoring Maurice's protests that it was none of their business.

Doug chose to answer. "No, I'm not."

"Divorced? Widowed? Aren't you ever lonely"

Victor was about to tell the ever-nosy Johnnie to back off when Doug surprised him by answering. "I've never been married, but I have been lonely. I have always imagined I might find happiness in a committed relationship, but it seems I have not been fortunate so far."

"Ah, yes. Loneliness, hmmm?" Johnnie may have been about to grill Doug further, or launch into a tale of personal woe, when Maurice cut in.

"Sometimes I'd give anything for a moment of true loneliness." He glared at Johnnie in a manner that clearly said butt out.

"I look very dashing in black, Maury. Just try me."

"It does seem, sometimes," Doug interjected quickly, distracting the lovers from their impending quarrel, "that time passes and our expectations are never met. It's as if we are heading toward a desired destination, but we travel and travel and yet never quite arrive." He thumbed his eyebrow, staring at the empty table across the aisle from them.

"Yeah." Victor added. "Sometimes you know someone and then lose touch with them. They stay young in your head until the next time you see them, it's a shock. They got older. Makes you realize that you got older too." He sighed and stirred his coffee with his fork. "And sometimes you hear that someone you once knew is dead. And then you run into them again six months later. Is that freaky or what?"

There were shivers all around the table. "That has, indeed, happened to me, once. I had a friend, when I was young —" Doug said.

"What I'm thinking is," Victor continued right over Doug's words, unable to stop himself. "Who the hell has all the answers? I mean, I wouldn't be here if I had all the answers, you know? Well, not here, here." He gestured around the restaurant. "But here, this stage of my life, like."

"Or would you?" Johnnie mused. "That's the question, isn't it?"

"Right. Right." Something in this conversation appealed to Victor. He could really relate to what they were saying. "You can't run away from your past, 'cause it's in you. It *is* you. Sometimes it's like a book, you know. Simple. One event, one turning point makes you who and what you are in life. It all turns from there. Like this." Victor held up his fork, dripping coffee back into his cup. "Like one of these. In the road."

Doug watched him with cautious interest. Maurice made encouraging noises. Johnnie opened his mouth to speak, but all that came out was an *oomph*, almost as if he'd been kicked under the table. Victor wondered why the fuck he was telling this story.

"We were both 17. I was so in love I could taste it. She thought we were just good friends. Had a thing for the captain of the football team, you know?" He glanced at Doug who just nodded, encouraging him to carry on with his story. Victor returned his eyes to his fork, now spattering coffee on the table as he flipped it back and forth.

"We were in this supermarket. My mom had asked me to get some milk or something." He shrugged, although it might have been a little on the shudder-y side. "Otherwise why would two seventeen-year-olds be in a grocery story? Funny, I remember the song that was playing on somebody's radio, right over the store's crappy Muzak. It was *Space Cowboy* by Steve Miller. Remember it?" Victor hummed the song softly, his fork beating rhythm on the laminate tabletop. His humming clashed badly with the whiny alternative rock tune playing on the restaurant's sound system, though. When no one commented on his musical memories, he continued.

"So she says to me, 'I think that man has a gun,' and I panic and yell, 'Gun!' Which makes the robber panic and he yells at everyone to get down on the floor, now. Now!" Victor's voice grew deep and husky as he instinctively mimicked the voice of the robber from his memory and his nightmares. He couldn't take his eyes off the fork now, gripping it in one white-knuckled hand and polishing it, polishing it with his thumb.

"My friend, she's near the customer service desk — and by the way, they should have called it the customer *dis*service desk. Once when I...no, right, right. One story at a time.

"So my friend ducks behind the customer service desk — throws herself, really, knocking the telephone set down with her. Deliberately.

"Now the robber, he goes over to some little old lady and screaming at her, 'Get up! Go get the cash and fill this bag. Now!'" Victor's voice shook. So did he, a bit. The fork now shone almost as if wet, not unlike Victor's eyes.

"So the robber is watching the little old lady go from one register to the next, dumping the cash into his loot bag."

"What about your friend and the phone?" Johnnie asked.

"She could have stayed down and out of sight, but no, she's got to be the hero. Seventeen years old and she dials 9-1-1, whispering about what's happening to the cops."

"Where were you, Victor?" Doug encouraged gently.

"I was kneeling behind the Coke machine, probably safer than anyone else. I felt so guilty about that; that I was safe while the girl I was crazy about was busy being the hero."

Victor let go of the fork and ran a hand across his clammy forehead. "He couldn't see me. I was safe. But I could see everything in one of those round shoplifting mirrors."

Johnnie moved his hand soothingly up and down Victor's neck.

"I really wanted to save her. It seemed like my duty. But I was so scared. So scared. I mean, he had a gun and all. I'd never even held a gun back then."

There was silence at the table; the background noise of the other diners seemed far away, in another place, another time.

Victor couldn't believe he was saying all this. To Doug. Here. Today. But he couldn't stop himself, either. It all just came tumbling out, spilling out on the table like the sugar had earlier — granules of his life spread out for everyone to see.

He wanted to stop, to shut up about his inglorious past, but all eyes were on him, silently waiting for the conclusion to the story, the pivotal point of his entire life. Words tumbled from his mouth, bypassing his better judgment altogether.

"Then the robber guy must have heard something, so he rushes over to the customer service counter and drags my friend out by her arm. He figures out instantly what she's doing, gets on the phone and tries to tell the operator that it's a prank being pulled by a kid who's just angry she got caught shoplifting cigarettes. From his side of the conversation, it sounds like the operator believes him and is about to cancel the call.

"My friend, though, she's got some sort of martyr complex, so she starts screaming it's a lie, that he's the bad guy. He lets go of her arm and backhands her, hard. She goes flying into the counter. Had bruises for weeks after that.

"When he hit her, I finally grew some balls and charged out from my hiding place, planting myself right between him and the exit. I start screaming that it's a holdup, hoping the operator will hear. A few of the others hostages start yelling too, so the operator gets the picture.

"At this point, the cops arrive. What we find out after is that they got the call from the dispatcher saying it's a prank, but protocol says they got to check it out anyway. So just two cops, coming in the front door. Seeing the situation, the robber starts to run. And since I'm in his way, he heads right for me, thinking he'll just shove the skinny kid out of his way and make a clean getaway.

"He comes at me like a bull in Pamperloma or wherever the fuck those idiots run with bulls. And I get out of his way. I just fucking throw myself to the floor like a coward."

"You were seventeen, Victor. It was okay to be scared." Maurice said. "It's what they instruct employees to do. They have theft insurance."

"There was no need for you to take on the role of police officer, Victor," Doug added.

"No, but my friend has the balls to call 9-1-1, and here's me, I don't even stick out a foot to try and trip him." Victor's guts twisted painfully. He deeply regretted his large sandwich as the taste of goat cheese swims a little at the back of his throat, the flavor notably unchanged even after sitting in his stomach for half an hour. He grabbed Doug's water, swallowing noisily, giving Johnnie a chance to get a word in.

"So the guy got away because of you." Johnnie truly believed he was helping. Maurice may have kicked him under the table again. So might Doug. Either way, he abruptly closed his mouth on whatever other helpful comments he had planned to make.

"No, actually," Victor took up the story again. "The robber actually got caught because of me."

"What?"

"Huh?"

"Please elaborate."

"It all happened so fast: the cops came in, the robber bolted, I got out of his way, and he slipped on something where I'd been standing and went down like a ton of pricks."

Victor raised his head and looked pleadingly at Doug, almost unaware of Johnnie, who was still rubbing Victor's neck, and Maurice, silent and patient.

"One cop rushed over to subdue the alleged criminal while the other radioed for backup and checked out the situation. The cops yelled details back and forth to each other across the store so nobody could miss it. The cop who's busy cuffing the bad guy reports in." And here Victor adopted a very serious, yet mocking tone: "'The alleged perpetrator appears to have slipped on a puddle of urine.' The other cop yells, 'What?' And the first cop yells back, 'The kid pissed himself.' You know, real loud just so everybody knows I'm...I'm not just a coward, I'm a pissant."

Victor waited for the inevitable comments, now that he'd reached the climax of his life-altering story.

"Oh God, Victor. I certainly hope you weren't wearing light-colored pants." Victor glared and pulled away from Johnnie's soothing hand.

"I don't think pissant means what you think it does," was Doug's only comment.

"How does it end?"

"They all figured I'd done it on purpose. You know, like a seventeen-year-old could plan ahead like that." A tiny bit of triumph filled Victor's soul. Triumph and guilt intertwined, as it did every time he'd had to tell that story — to the police, to their parents, to the marriage counselor. "I was commended by

the police and the store manager for such a clever maneuver."
He'd never told anyone he hadn't done it deliberately.

"So, did you get the girl?" Johnnie asked, dodging the swat
from across the table.

"Yeah. I got the girl. That was Yolanda, my wife. Ex-wife
now." And Maurice's boss, which was how he'd met Maurice
and then Johnnie in the first place. *Why, oh why, am I saying this
stuff*, Victor silently wondered.

"She married you even after…you know. That?" Good old
Johnnie. Think it and speak it. Shoe leather is his favorite flavor.

Victor leaned back in the booth, chewed on the side of his
thumbnail for a moment. "Yup. She thought I was a hero." He
nodded at their looks of disbelief. "She thinks I staged the
pissing thing as a distraction and a way of foiling his getaway.
That I was willing to embarrass myself to save her." The looks
didn't change. "To this very day she thinks I did it for her." So
my marriage was based on a lie — no wonder it failed. He kept
the last to himself.

The silence that followed Victor's oversharing moment was
awkward and lengthy. The waitress finally arrived with coffee
refills and Johnnie began another story, this one involving
patent leather pumps, a pair of Australian dykes, and a stuffed
moose. Victor couldn't recall a single detail later.

There was a brief struggle between Maurice and Doug when
the bill arrived. Maurice insisted on paying, explaining that, as a
lawyer, he could not only afford it, but expense it as well. He
worked at Summerwood and Summerwood, Yolanda's family's
law firm. He began to explain the areas of law they practiced,
his narrative distracting Doug long enough for Maurice to
snatch the bill away. Victor thought it divine justice that
Yolanda's firm was picking up the tab for his date. Not a date.
Not a date, he rebuked himself.

But when Doug asked to check the bill for accuracy, saying
that he was, after all, an accountant, Victor saw him slip forty
dollars into the bill presenter. As good as his word, Doug had
indeed bought Victor's lunch. Victor watched Maurice's

knowing and exasperated look when the credit card receipt came back to him for signature, obviously made out for the balance less the forty dollars.

Eventually, the group exited the booth and the restaurant, but not before Doug and Victor agreed to go out with Johnnie and Maurice the following Friday night — a double date, Johnnie teased. "We'll think of something entertaining for four beautiful men to do on a spring evening." Maurice said he'd call with details and followed his departing partner toward The Bay and its semiannual scratch'n'save event.

Back on their quest for a decent pair of running shoes, Victor shopped like he was on a mission from God. He dragged Doug to Athletes World, Footlocker and SportChek, which were spread out just about equidistant around the huge mall. He interrogated the minimum-wage clerks mercilessly, asking them technical questions that were well beyond their limited levels of expertise and of interest. He insisted Doug try on pair after pair until he finally hustled him back to Athletes World and bought the second pair he'd tried on.

"I fail to see much difference between these and the pair I have been running in. Aside from the extra seventy-five dollars."

"Running's both an art and a science, Doug. This is the science part."

"Ah."

"Want to try 'em out?"

"Well, yes. I suppose I should. I'll see you at the gym tomorrow, then."

"No, wait. Hold up. I mean let's go for a run together. We both have to do it anyway." To Doug's raised eyebrow he said, "My gym stuff's in the trunk. We'll change at your place so you can get your stuff and run up in your neck of the woods. Ever been to Sherwood Park?"

The stark basement studio apartment surprised Victor. Surely an accountant could afford more than this stuffy little hole. There was an impressive computer setup in one corner and inexpensive Ikea bookshelves along two walls crowded with well-ordered books: mainly tax law and accounting procedures, but plenty of old volumes as well: fiction, science, philosophy. At Doug's polite cough, Victor turned to his host. "You sure have a lot of books there, Doug."

"As I mentioned previously, my grandparents were attached to a world literacy organization. We moved around a lot and I had few opportunities to make friends as a young lad. Books became my companions." Victor felt sad for the lonely youth Doug was describing. Doug moved toward the shelves and ran a hand fondly along the spines of a few treasured volumes. Maybe Doug had been bookish, enjoying his subdued childhood. Victor pictured a studious young man, pale and frail, pouring over great tomes with proud grandparents looking on.

"So just you and your books, eh, Doug?"

"When I wasn't playing hockey, at Boy Scouts, learning to hunt, fish and track, being home-schooled, and helping my grandparents both in their mobile library and around the house, learning local native languages as well as Cantonese and a bit of Mandarin, yes. Then it was just my books and me."

Oh. Busy kid. Victor had played a lot of basketball as a kid. Danced and boxed, too. No hunting, though, unless you count his early and relentless pursuit of Yolanda. He shook his head to clear it. Here he was in the apartment of this hot new guy, the bed mere feet away, and he was thinking of Yolanda. It was all Johnnie's fault. He quickly stripped off his T-shirt, tossing it on the precisely made bed.

"What are you doing, Victor?" Dismay was evident in Doug's tone.

"Getting changed to go running. Why?" Victor went with innocent. "Make you nervous, there? Don't be, you've changed with me before." Then he realized that while he showered and changed at the gym without a second thought, he'd never seen Doug less than fully clothed. "You want I should go into the bathroom to change and you can change out here?"

"No need, Victor. You are, after all, the guest." Doug whipped behind a door that Victor assumed was the bathroom. A moment later he called through the door, "Are you decent yet, Victor?"

"Decent? I'm way better than that. Some say I'm amazing." Reenacting the first day they'd met, Doug emerged just in time to see Victor adjusting himself in his spandex running shorts.

"Oh, dear." Doug scrutinized his new running shoes, scratching his eyebrow a few times; the stitches were gone, but the fading red line would no doubt turn white and remain for life. He must have figured Victor was fully clothed a minute later when he lifted his head and announced, "I need to collect my Jack."

That struck Victor as so odd that he didn't even bother to ask. He just followed along to a neighboring apartment, assuming "collect my Jack" was some sort of slang expression, quite possibly the northern equivalent of "spank the monkey" or "choke the chicken." He was forcefully reminded of Doug's literal-mindedness when twenty-or-so pounds of pure muscle threw itself on his chest. He stumbled backward, losing his balance and landing surprised but unhurt on the hallway floor. The dog took the opportunity to become intimate with Victor's face and neck, tongue-bathing him in a coating of saliva. Well, at least somebody was. "Get him off me! Get him off!"

Doug tried to comply, but the dog seemed proficient at ignoring him. By the time the dog was successfully convinced to leave Victor alone, Doug, Victor and neighbor-cum-dogsitter were in stitches.

"Victor, I'd like you to meet my neighbor, Mr. Nbizzlemeiner."

"Pleezed to meet chew. Call me Asilindadabe."

"Likewise," Victor mumbled as they shook hands.

"And this is Jack. He's a Jack Russell Terrier. And he seems to have taken quite a shine to you."

Jack raised a paw, but Victor kept his distance, waving back instead. Jack lay down on the grimy hall carpet, muzzle on paws, gazing at Victor and whining piteously.

"I sink eet's luff," Mr. Nbizzlemeiner pronounced — badly.

"I'm a lovable guy," Victor agreed.

"Or maybe it's worms." Doug looked thoughtful as they headed out to Victor's car and drove to their run.

※ ※ ※

Victor was impressed at how much Doug had improved already. The initial fitness report had said he'd barely been able to finish the full mile test. Maybe running on cross-country terrain was easier for him than running on a treadmill: more air, or something. Doug was able to do the complete circuit through the woods twice before he collapsed, gasping, on a handy park bench.

Jack roamed around the open area in front of their chosen bench, greeting dog after dog as their owners paraded them by.

"Sure are a lot of yuppie puppies here. You really have to watch where you step in spite of the stoop and scoop laws."

"There are a limited number —" Doug gasped. "Of off-leash parks in this city." Doug wheezed. "I believe people travel here from quite a large —" Doug panted. "Catchment area."

Victor grinned evilly as he watched the third consecutive dog owner swat at Jack as he tried to mount yet another canine beauty, seeming to consider the height differential irrelevant to the ways of love.

"Why don't you fix your dog?" the overprotective owner yelled in their direction.

Doug hung his head, blushing, saying softly, apparently to his new footwear, "I feel, sometimes as if I'm more his than he's mine. I wouldn't want him to make that choice for me."

Ah, projecting, are we? Victor thought, then commented aloud, "He certainly is friendly." Jack was currently trying to mount a full-size poodle with an elaborate haircut and a furious owner.

Having regained his composure somewhat, Doug straightened on the bench. "Jack was raised in the north. There weren't many dogs around up there, and those that were, were pack animals and working dogs. He fit in fine up there, being rather a scrapper. I'm afraid he is very much out of his element here in an urban environment, and doesn't seem to be able to relate to a flexible pack structure. I believe he's confused, and I feel I must be patient while he works through his issues."

The unrepentant dog appeared at their side. Victor could have sworn he was laughing.

"Yeah, Doug. That's probably it. Or could just be your dog's a slut." And they say pets grow to be like their owners. Too bad it wasn't the other way round. The second dog Jack had tried to mount had been male.

Jack yapped, whined, and snarled.

"Yes. I suppose highly adaptive would be another term for it." It appeared to Victor that Doug was actually addressing the dog.

The Ego Has Landed

The following Friday evening after work, Doug and Victor met up with Johnnie and Maurice as arranged.

After a pleasant dinner at a cozy authentic Italian restaurant at the foot of Jarvis Street, they found themselves wandering up Church. Victor had been surprised and amused when he'd picked up one of those colorful but not-to-scale maps of the city and it actually listed Church as "The heart of Toronto's Gay Ghetto."

Victor was a little embarrassed when the third guy passed them wearing an outfit almost identical to his. What had he been thinking, wearing a Castro-style sleeveless shirt? And he was kind of warm in the black-jeans-and-boots thing he always had going on. He'd have to slash a pair into cut-offs this year if it got as hot as predicted. The weather people foretold a scorching summer, and Doug said something about bark and moss and caterpillars wearing wool confirming it. Or was that how to tell which way was north? Doug was a fountain of information, useful and otherwise. Victor just loved to hear him talk. Sometimes he even listened.

Still thinking about clothing choices, Victor appraised Johnnie and Maurice. It was handy that Johnnie worked in the fashion industry; they always were on the cutting edge of classic good taste. Both wore tailored slacks in a lightweight fabric, Johnnie in khaki and the more conservative Maurice in navy. Johnnie looked fine in a cotton-knit short-sleeved sweater, while his partner sported a hemp shirt that would have been illegal in the States. If you can't smoke it, wear it. Or vice versa, the key word being vice.

Victor figured tasteful fashion was okay for some, but he preferred his own classic style — the best of the '70s, '80s and '90s. In his opinion, he'd yet to see anything good come out of the 2000s, though.

"You know how they have the signs in Chinatown in Chinese as well as English?" Johnnie posed the question to the others in general, but only Doug acknowledged his comment. "And on the Danforth, the signs are in Greek as well as English?" Again Johnnie waited for his audience to react. "So why aren't the signs around this area...well, pink or rainbow-colored or something?"

"Yeah, Johnnie. I've so often wondered about that myself," Victor cut in, hoping to head off any request for clarification from his "date." Obviously, Doug was cool with all this, but Victor was just a little nervous about being too in-your-face with it.

"I've been thinking about colors myself, lately," Maurice mused. "We seem to have pretty much appropriated them all, I'm afraid."

"Okay, I'll bite." Knowing Maurice, Victor figured he was going somewhere with this. "What do you mean, Maury?"

"Well, originally we were assigned pink, right?" This from Johnnie, so he must have heard it before.

"Right." Maurice took back the floor, or, in this case, sidewalk. "And then we pretty much took all the pastels."

"Nobody else wanted them after the early '60s, anyway." Their tandem storytelling seemed almost as if they'd rehearsed it.

"Then we managed to appropriate the entire rainbow."

"Not to mention black, because black is always cool."

"And white, because it really shows off a tan and makes a room look larger."

"So, what," Maurice asked, "does that leave for the straight boys to wear?"

"Brown, I assume," sighed Doug, stepping forward, his tan Dockers and mud-colored polo shirt making his point for him. He made a deep and elegant bow, right down to his brown loafers.

Victor grinned at this bit of impromptu street theater. He felt contented and happy and very much pleased with the evening. He slung a friendly arm around Doug, the two glasses of wine with dinner perhaps responsible for the brief nuzzle and low, throaty "Looks good on you, Doug. Looks good on you."

Doug leaned into the one-armed hug, even returning it. Not wanting to press his luck, Victor stepped away, removing his arm from Doug's shoulder before Doug could do so; it doesn't count as rejection if you orchestrate it yourself, right?

On this unusually warm late spring evening, many of the establishments along the street had their windows and doors open. As they passed a small dance club that tended to attract a more mature crowd, the strains of "It's Raining Men" leeched out onto the patio and surrounding sidewalk.

"Ooo. I love this song. Come on. Let's go dance before it's over." Johnnie grabbed Maurice's hand and dragged his protesting partner into the club and onto the dance floor. Victor and Doug followed with reservations, after informing the doorman they didn't have any. They managed to find a relatively quiet spot at a small standing-height bar to one side of the room. It was scarcely more than a laminated arm rest, a place for drinks and elbows. They could even sort of see the dance floor when the early evening crowd parted just so.

"What'll it be, guys?" Great service, Victor thought, till he turned to see the waiter posing in front of Doug. The young Denzel look-alike held his tray aloft in a way that flexed his bicep to great advantage. The skimpy Tommy Hilfiger tank top showcased his lean, muscular chest, which was mere centimeters from Doug's.

Doug informed him that they probably wouldn't be staying long enough to enjoy a refreshing beverage. Victor waited for him to finish and ordered three Sleeman's beers and a lemonade, knowing from experience that it would be quite some time before their dancing fool friends grew weary and came in search of them. He figured with service the way it was in these kinds of places, their nice cold drinks should just be arriving by then. He grinned at Doug and began tapping out a light tattoo in counterpoint on the countertop.

"Fire!" the Ohio Players screamed in retro-disco frenzy. Succumbing to a wave of atavistic compulsion, Victor bumped his hip into Doug's, spun around and bumped Doug's hip again with his other one.

"Would you like to go dance, Victor?"

"What? Huh? With you?" Tapping feet and rolling hips stilled, he stared open-mouthed at his friend. "I mean, of course I'd like to dance with you, Doug. I just never thought…" Why was Doug looking dismayed? He'd made the damn offer.

"Oh, no. I didn't mean with me. I don't…that is to say, I don't really dance. Not very well. At all." He babbled, nervously, raising his voice enough to be heard over the music. His cuticles suddenly seemed to absorb all his attention.

"So it's not the guy thing, then, it's the dancing thing?"

Doug nodded. "In many cultures, including the Greek, Israeli, Irish, the men always dance together. Why, even square dancing here in North America…"

"You got a point there, Doug?"

"Please, Victor. I know you've said how much you enjoy dancing. I'm sure there are many people here who would be only too pleased to dance with you."

"You sure? Cause I don't like leaving you here if you're not comfortable with it. You've been a hell of a sport about it all up to now." Even as he was saying all the right things, Victor was eyeing the crowd for a suitable dance partner. It was killing him to be standing on the sidelines — he just wasn't made that way.

A last quick glance at Doug, who assured him again he'd be fine — that someone had to stay and pay for the drinks when they arrived — and Victor was off to join Johnnie and Maurice on the floor. He tossed, "Can't get down if you don't get up!" back over his shoulder at the nodding and smiling and somewhat confused Doug.

Victor was a great dancer, and after five minutes of boogying with Johnnie and Maurice, he was the hit of the dance floor. He did the machine gun, the bus stop, and since it was retro-disco night, he even borrowed Johnnie and did the hustle, Maurice being only too happy to stand at the sidelines and catch his breath for a tune or two.

From the corner of his eye, Victor noted one or two interesting — and apparently interested — men checking him out. None of them as interesting as Doug, though. And speaking of Doug, he'd left him alone for probably way too long now. He executed a graceful spin that ended with him facing the corner where he'd left his friend. And stopped dead. Doug was smiling warmly — no, delightedly — up at a tall man, who stood, back to Victor, far, far too close to his Doug.

Victor flew from the dance floor and crossed to the bar with great ground-eating strides, the crowd parting for him as he passed. He stepped up to the infatuated pair and got a seriously dirty look from the big man, whom he now recognized as some sports celebrity. Basketball? Lacrosse? Curling? Some Canadian sport. God, the guy was in shape. And big. Did he mention big?

"Shit! I wanted to get you alone," the athlete half-joked to Doug, half-hinted for Victor to leave.

Trying for vaguely civil, Victor replied in kind. "Thanks. Way to make a guy feel wanted."

"Victor!" Doug exclaimed, shining eyes full on the other man. Victor had gotten used to having Doug's laser-like attention all to himself. This he did not like in the least. "This is Yves Timmons. Yves, this is Victor Brighton." Doug looked so enamored of Timmons that Victor was surprised he remembered his own name, let alone Victor's.

"Right. Right. The hockey player. What brings you here?" The polite words said, "stay"; the tone said, "fuck off."

"Same thing as you, buddy. Cruising. Hoping to get lucky. What? You think they don't let fags play in the NHL?" He laughed short and sharp. "When you're as good as I am, they'll turn a blind eye to anything."

Doug's smile, like the setting sun, faded a bit. "I never really…" His mouth snapped closed on his words as Timmons ran a rough hand down his cheek.

"So what's your name, good-looking?"

Doug froze, a look of disbelief on his face. "You don't…you don't remember me?"

"I can't say I do. Did we fuck before? I think I would have remembered you." Timmons let his hand run down Doug's neck, shoulder, chest, where he toyed with one nipple through the thin summer-weight shirt. Doug gave his aggressor a halfhearted shove, succeeding only in shifting the substantial Timmons a little to one side.

Persistent, Timmons purred as he moved in to rub himself against Doug's hip. "Like that, do you?"

"Okay, hockey boy, that's enough body checking. You're not on the ice now." Victor's voice, full of outrage, cut through the music like a knife.

"Fuck off. He's not protesting." Timmons dismissed Victor with a wave, not bothering to look at him.

Victor moved to stand by Doug's free side; from the corner of his eye he saw the sweaty Johnnie and Maurice arrive and freeze, taking in the strange tableau. "You want this, buddy?" Victor asked Doug softly. "You okay?"

Every insecurity Victor had ever had echoed through his head. Of course Doug would want this hockey legend; who wouldn't? A nasty little voice that lived just below Victor's confidence suggested that it was never that Doug wasn't interested in men, it was only that Doug wasn't interested in him. Victor's throat tightened a little. He wondered if he was having an anaphylactic reaction to the shrimp he'd had for dinner. Or maybe he was allergic to heartache.

Doug looked miserably at the floor. Okay. Victor didn't need any more answer than that. He steeled himself and placed one hand on Timmons' shoulder, pushing slightly. "Off, Timmons. Now. I'm not saying it twice."

"No. If he doesn't want a piece of this MVP, he'd better tell me himself." His words were directed at Victor, but his eyes never left Doug's downturned face.

"Look, he's saying no. Get it now? Or you take one too many pucks to the head?" Victor got himself all up in Timmons's face, trying to wedge his own body between Doug and his assailant. "Back off, Timmons, or I'm going to drop you like Grade 10 French."

"Oh. So that's it. It's not pretty boy here you want. It's this, eh?" He chuckled and turned just enough that he was no longer pressed against Doug, but facing Victor instead, all up close and personal. "Do I have to go through you to get him? Because I will if you really, really beg." Shit-eating did not begin to describe the smug look on Timmons's chops.

"That's right, asshole. You do gotta go through me. And I want a piece a' you, all right. Just not that piece." He glanced scathingly toward the other man's groin. "You want to step outside, I guarantee you that nose of yours'll finally get broken. No NHL refs anywhere in sight to take me outta the game! I'll be all over you like white on snow." Victor's voice climbed a notch as his tirade continued. "Believe me, it will not be pretty and neither will you when I get done with you!"

Timmons backed up by baby steps as Victor bore down on him in full rant.

"Okay, buddy. Okay. Keep your shorts on. I'll leave you two lovebirds alone. You deserve each other." It might have just occurred to Timmons that he was being turned down. "It's your loss, fuckhead. And his loss, too." He jerked his chin at the still frozen Doug. "I'm outta here." He turned to leave, flushed and angry. Doug raised his head, a mixture of loss and shame etched on his handsome face. Next to him, one of the gawking spectators put a match to her cigarette, illuminating Doug's profile clearly.

Timmons froze, staring at Doug. "Douggie?" Timmons's tones were suddenly soft and incredulous. He took a hesitant step back toward Doug, glancing warily at the still bristling Victor.

Doug nodded, looking miserable.

"Doug!" Timmons repeated, a bit of warmth creeping into his voice.

"You know this guy?" Victor asked suspiciously, gaze swinging from one to the other.

Doug didn't answer. Timmons, however, seemed under the impression that Victor was addressing him. He moved possessively back into Doug's space. "Yeah. We know each other. Real well. Isn't that right, Douggie?" A nasty little chuckle, then, "Your boyfriend here doesn't know you've been fucked by the best forward in the NHL?" He traced a finger along Doug's cheekbone, then turned to Victor, grinning evilly. "Oh, yeah. I've had his pretty little ass. I was his first, in fact. And maybe, if he's lucky, I'll do him again tonight. Do both of you, maybe. You're not a bad looker yourself. I got a thing for feisty. I could go for a *ménage à moi.*"

Doug snapped out of whatever fog he'd been inhabiting, straightening to full height, but still several centimeters shorter than Timmons. "That's quite enough, Yves."

"Oh. So you've developed a spine after all these years — more than just something for me to bite while I'm fucking you."

Doug's fist flew toward his antagonist. Victor anticipated the move and caught it on his own palm, softening the blow only slightly as the hand-wrapped fist landed on Timmons's jaw. The bastard flailed about uncoolly for several seconds before toppling like a felled tree, landing on his ass. Onlookers expecting a fight were sorely disappointed as he sat stunned for a moment. He started screaming obscenities and threats as he began hauling his bulk back up.

The word "lawsuit" had barely formed on Timmons's lips before Maurice in full lawyer mode was there with a soothing but implacable spiel and a business card, making it all go away. He gently helped Timmons to his feet and led him off to a quiet corner where they could talk privately.

Not bothering to watch Timmons's retreat, Victor turned to where Johnnie was trying to deal with the shaken and shaking Doug Newkirk. "I'm fine. I'm fine," he kept insisting, but when Johnnie reached out a gentle hand to touch his shoulder Doug shied away as if from a snake poised to strike.

Oh, fuck. And he'd seemed so cool with the whole fag trip. Fucking ego-tripping hockey fucker. Victor's inner voice was given to repetitive obscenity.

"That'll be $14.50." With great timing, the absentee waiter and their drinks finally materialized.

"I'll get it," Johnnie said. For once, Doug made no move to reach for his wallet, just stared somewhere around Victor's chest.

Victor approached Doug like he would a frightened animal, slowly, no sudden moves, speaking in soothing tones. "It's okay. Doug. Buddy. Can I take you out of here? Take you somewhere quiet? Somewhere safe?"

"I'm fine, Victor. I'm not a child." Oh. Doug being snarky; first time for that. Was that a good sign or bad? "I'd just like to get out of here, please. I'm sorry if this little contretemps has spoiled the evening."

"Don't worry 'bout it. Not your fault. Let's go, Doug. We'll see you later." He nodded when the returning Maurice made first a thumbs up gesture, then held his hand to his ear thumb up, finger toward mouth in the universal sign for *call me*. Victor slung an arm loosely over Doug's shoulders as they cut through the crowd, somewhat reassured when Doug seemed to shrink against him rather than shying away as he had from Johnnie's touch a moment ago.

Luckily they'd been heading back to the car when they stopped into the nightclub, so the parking lot was just behind the row of converted Victorian brownstones that housed the bar. He guided Doug to the GTO, glad this was an area of town where he could have his arm around another man without getting any flak.

Once they'd settled in the car, Victor asked again if Doug was all right.

He'd expected to be snapped at again — hell, he probably would have snapped too if someone was fussing at him like that. He was surprised that Doug sounded, well, not normal, but at least halfway human: "No. I'm, um, okay. Well, I'm not, of course, but I will be." The shaking came and went in waves. Victor had seen it before, been trained how to handle it.

"Okay. I'll take you home, then. Okay?"

"No. Not home. I…" Doug took a big gulp of air. Victor watched as he struggled to fill his lungs. "Yes, of course. I'm so sorry, Victor."

Victor knew a thing or two about trauma. "You don't want to go home, you don't have to go home. How 'bout my place? You want to come over for a while?" Concerned how this might sound, he added, "We can, um, watch movies or something until you feel better."

"Yes. I'd like that. Thanks." The acceptance without further dance of polite protest seemed very out of character for Doug. Victor kept one eye on traffic and one on his companion during the drive home.

✕ ✕ ✕

By the time they'd climbed the stairs to Victor's third-floor walk-up, Doug had begun to relax a bit. Victor stepped into his apartment and threw his arms wide, knocking his wrist painfully into the doorframe; but he never flinched, that would have ruined the effect. "Tada! Welcome to Chez Brighton." He was pleased to see Doug's mouth curve up just the slightest bit at the corners. Striding to the fridge, he peered inside. "What's your pleasure? We have beer, orange juice, hot chocolate. You can have one or all — whatever your little heart desires."

"I actually think I'd like a beer, please, Victor." This surprised Victor more than Doug agreeing to come home with him. Doug had made it clear early on that he didn't drink. Victor couldn't figure if he was a recovering alkie or a religious fundamentalist. Doug had said at the time that he just didn't like the taste and what it did to his head. Claimed he had a very low tolerance for alcohol. Well, he wasn't a child, as he'd said, and he was certainly entitled to a little ol' beer given the circumstances, whatever the hell they were. *I will not ask. I will not ask.* Victor couldn't wait to ask.

Victor plunked down on the sofa next to his guest, placing the two sweating bottles on the coffee table. He grabbed the remote and started flicking through channels, saying softly, "You let me know when you're ready to talk about it, 'kay?"

Doug nodded, hand on his beer and eyes on the flickering screen.

They ended up watching about three-quarters of an old black and white chick flick, both sniffing slightly when the ghost came back at the end for Mrs. Muir. Doug squeezed the bridge of his nose and began to make departing motions. He asked Victor if he could use the phone to call a taxi.

"Hey. I'll drive you. It's early yet." A glance at the VCR told him it was *12:00, 12:00, 12:00…* It felt around eleven thirty.

"It's a work night for you. And I've already kept you from doing whatever you would be doing with this time. I couldn't ask you for a ride home, as well. You've been most generous to include me in your evening with your friends at all and then I —"

Victor rested his chin on his hand, bracing his elbow on one knee. He lowered the volume on the TV and waited.

Doug fidgeted. Then moved around. Then re-settled himself on the couch. Eventually, he took a deep breath. "He was my best friend." Victor nodded: go on. "But he didn't recognize me tonight — not at first anyway. After all we'd been through together." He ran a shaky hand across his eyes.

"We were both sixteen the year my grandparents and I moved to Kapuskasing in northern Ontario, but we were already young men; you grow up fast in the north. He was going to be an NHL player and I was going to apply to the RCMP."

More encouraging and sympathetic noises from Victor.

"For once my grandparents stayed in one place long enough for me to attend regular public school with the other young people; I was home-schooled more often than not." Doug worried at the scar in his eyebrow.

"Yves and I were practically inseparable. Oddly, we had a long, hot — well for us, anyway — summer that year. Two long months of no school, no snow, no ice."

"Sounds good to me," Victor commented.

Doug shook his head. "No ice means no hockey. We didn't have an indoor rink, just pond hockey. Yves and I were at a loss to entertain ourselves that summer. And two hormonally challenged teenage boys, living in an isolated community with a deficiency of teenage girls, will find ways to get into trouble." He raised his gaze from his clenched hands to meet Victor's eyes, allowing Victor to draw his own conclusions.

"So you and he…?"

Doug nodded. "He was an exceedingly aggressive young man — he would need to be to have come so far in the highly competitive field of professional hockey. I suppose it only followed that he would be very…sexually aggressive as well."

"Penalty for high sticking." Victor attempted to introduce a bit of levity. He raised his hands in a gesture of apology at Doug's appalled look.

"I loved him, Victor. It was very serious to me. I don't love lightly."

"Sorry. Just getting in touch with my inner asshole."

"Humph. There's a lot of that going around tonight."

Ah. The return of Snarky Doug. Victor took that as a good sign.

"As I was saying." Doug's small glare in his direction warmed Victor slightly — talking was indeed helping. "I loved him completely: followed him around like a puppy. It was…difficult, but in retrospect, I doubt that he ever had similar feelings for me."

Not love Doug? How could anyone, given the opportunity, not love Doug?

"It ended badly, of course. There were fights, and small cruelties; it seemed to amuse him to see how far he could push me."

"A bored teenager is a bad teenager," Victor mused out loud. "Hey, I was a teenager myself once upon a time." It was the year I met Yolanda, he recalled, but this isn't about me.

"My grandmother was concerned about my intermittent sullen silences and angry outbursts; apparently we do have some history of instability in our family. I have this uncle… no, you're right. We don't need to get into that right now.

"Eventually we were found out and separated." Here Doug paused so long that Victor felt compelled to prod with another leading question. He felt like a cop interviewing a crime victim, and indeed, in some ways he was. "Were you caught all fragrant delectable?"

Doug started at that; a rueful smile prettied his face a bit. "You mean *in flagrante delicto?*"

"'S'what I said, isn't it?

Doug looked thoughtful. "No. Nothing so…so succinct."

"So how'd they find out?"

Doug reached up to rub his thumb across his left eyebrow, but was simultaneously driven to crack his neck sharply to the right, resulting in him gouging his eye with his own thumb. He took a moment to recover, then, with one eye slightly more red and weepy than the other, continued.

"My grandmother found blood on my underwear."

Victor gasped, but Doug hurriedly carried on, probably before Victor could ask any questions. *Penetrating* questions, Victor added mentally.

"I had a great deal of explaining to do. It was probably the last time in my life that I ever tried to hide any behavior of mine behind lies and deceit. I was sorely punished and his parents were informed — quietly, discreetly. The only reason the authorities were not brought into it was because sixteen is the age of legal majority in Ontario, so no actual crime had been committed. But even if one of us had been underage, I doubt my grandparents would have gone through any sort of official channels. They were of the old school that believed in not —"

"— airing your dirty laundry in public. I get it."

"Quite literally so."

He paused to take a sip of the beer that had been emptied an hour ago. Victor fetched them each another one without comment.

"I would have done anything for him. I loved him. I must have. I did…that."

"And by 'that' you mean…"

Doug nodded.

"And you found it…um, unpleasant?"

Doug nodded again. "Although I imagine being the…performer rather than the…recipient might have been less so."

"Performer? Oh. You mean you never…? He never…? Well, that's just not buddies."

"It was all right. It was what he wanted. I was happy to give of myself that way, despite the…discomfort." Doug shifted on the seat as if the mere memory caused him…discomfort.

"Hey," Victor's tone was hushed, soothing. "You know it doesn't have to be that way. It can be really, really good if you know what you're doing."

"Spare me the sales pitch, please." Doug's eyes blazed, his tone nasty. "Please," he added again, softer, firm but apologetic too.

Inside Victor bristled at the accusation, but knowing there was a kernel of truth in the caustic statement and knowing this was not the time, he apologized. "I'm sorry Doug. I'm just…really…fond of you."

"Well, be fond of me from the other end of the couch!" Doug snapped. "Don't think that one childhood transgression a sexual orientation makes."

Victor puzzled the odd wording for a minute.

"Have I ever said or done anything to make you think I was coming on to you — since that first night, I mean? Have I?"

Doug looked uncomfortable.

Victor pressed. "Well, have I?"

"Sometimes you…look at me."

"I look at you?"

"You look at me."

"Well, pardon me for wanting to be able to pick my friend out of a police lineup."

Doug's turn to look puzzled. "Now why would I be in a police lineup, Victor?"

"It's just an expression. Forget it, Doug. How does this Yves-the-dickhead story end?"

"After our affair was discovered, Yves was sent away to live with an aunt in Edmonton. It was probably better for his career in the long run. He would not have developed the necessary skills if he had only myself, and a few other local children to challenge him." He sipped the new beer, then rested the cool bottle on his forehead a moment before continuing.

"I was devastated at the loss of his companionship, and sank into what would probably be defined today as a bout of clinical depression. I gained a great deal of weight over the following months — weight I've had trouble shedding until quite recently. It was my weight that kept me out of the Mounties. Despite my best attempts — it was then I tried jogging — I was never able to pass the RCMP admissions requirements.

"At the time, I just stayed in my room and read, ate and slept for as many hours of the day as I could. My grandmother called it malingering and enrolled me in any extracurricular activities she could find. Although the mail was slow, I partook of a variety of math and science contests, and my lifelong affinity for numbers blossomed."

"So your star-crossed love affair with the boy next door turned into career choices for both of you. Almost sounds like a happy ending, Doug, except for the part where I want to beat the crap out of him for hurting you. No wonder you're so shook up. You know what I can't understand?"

He waited for Doug to look at him again.

"Given the way you kind of, well, fell apart there tonight, and now I know the history behind it, I don't get why you were so cool about giving me the brush-off that first night. With a plum 'n' all."

"With a…? What's fruit got to do…? Oh. Yes, of course. A plum."

"And fruit." Victor grinned.

Doug chuckled at Victor's play on words, his momentary confusion passing. "Hmmm. I hadn't really thought about it." Sounding surprised, he stared at his beer, and ran his thumb under one side of the label where the glue was starting to give with the condensation.

"I guess I didn't find you threatening. No, that's not any sort of insult. I mean it in a good way." His smile had a little life in it for the first time since running into puck-head. "And, of course, we don't have any history between us. Perhaps I haven't actually generalized the trauma to similar incidents — it requires the actual perpetrator to induce a posttraumatic stress-type response. Well, a mild one, perhaps, in relative terms, but I did seem rather…not myself."

"You ever see anyone about this? Talk to anyone? A professional, I mean." He didn't really expect Doug to answer this exceedingly personal question, but once again Doug surprised him.

"Yes. I suppose if I'd had more enlightened caregivers, they might have taken me to a psychiatrist at the time, but as I've said, my grandparents were rather old-fashioned in their approach to childrearing, and the nearest psychiatrist would have been several hundred kilometers away, although one could still apply to the Ministry of Health for Northern travel grants in those days." He paused, no doubt to see if Victor wanted to discuss government programming.

Victor made it clear he did not.

"It wasn't until much more recently that I decided to undertake a course of therapy with a trained medical professional."

"Yeah. I saw a guy for a while when me and Yolanda broke up. We'd seen this lady marriage counselor together, then when it didn't work out. Yolanda even got her in the settlement — next hardest thing I ever had to do was find my own shrink. Thank God they're covered by our health care setup here in Ontario." Victor leaned his head on the back of the sofa, raising one arm to wipe his brow, his metal watchband leaving uncomfortable red steaks across his forehead. "Guess that makes us a couple of loons, eh?"

"Interestingly," Doug continued as if he hadn't been interrupted, "my therapist said the reason I gained so much weight at that point in my life was to render myself unattractive, thereby avoiding any further encounters of a sexual or romantic nature. He felt it was a very good sign that I was able to lose the weight over the course of our treatment; that I was at last recovering from this childhood trauma, and perhaps even able to enter the world of social interaction again, this time armed with the coping tools of an adult."

This sounded promising to Victor, and he said so. He truly hoped that Doug would find someone with whom he'd be happy. And since Doug seemed bound and determined that he was straight, sexuality being very much a matter of personal taste, he assumed it wouldn't be one Victor Brighton any time soon.

Sighing, Victor retrieved an extra pillow and some blankets from the hall closet. He knew he should, as a well-raised host, offer his bed to Doug and insist he sleep on his own couch. He also knew that Doug would argue about it, so he bypassed the entire discussion and just tossed the bedding to his friend. He didn't even consider inviting Doug to share his bed; not after what had gone down this evening. Besides, he had a lot to think about tonight, and for once was happy just to sleep on it.

Victor considered his steroids investigation very much a part of his job description at Orr's Gym. Despite the crappy way his not-date had gone with Veronica a few weeks ago, he was glad she'd asked him to do the snooping around. He now felt he had official sanction to pursue this line of inquiry.

He made a point of being a friend to all comers, working hard to build trust and ingratiate himself with the various subcultures who spent mega-time at the gym: the gays who lived in the area, the yuppies who worked in the nearby central business district, and the kids who partied in the local nightclubs and bars. Then there was the leftover chunk of individuals who fit into none of these categories, coming downtown just to work out or for a hundred other reasons. Downtown: something for every lifestyle. And although sometimes Victor felt like he had no life, he always had style!

He was everywhere around the gym, like a one-man posse, joining conversations, dispensing advice, asking leading questions. Several times people had gotten him alone and tried to market steroids to him, although they weren't selling directly. Some mysterious "Big Boss" had introduced a sort of pyramid marketing scheme whereby each person was a cell in a fifth-column type of organization. The low-ranking sellers Victor made contact with were unaware of the identity of the guy at the top.

A couple of times Victor's well-dropped hints led to conversations that began, "Er, no, actually. I'm looking to score some myself." Victor could have put group B in touch with group A, but that would have made him party to the illegal sales of steroids, so he just shrugged and moved on. If people thought him poorly connected and out of the loop, he'd just have to live with that. He couldn't afford to have any incriminating activity on his record.

One difficult conversation went something like, "No. Ha ha. I'm not trying to muscle in on anyone's territory. Does that mean you've got some to sell? Hey! Come back here!"

About once a week, Victor hung around till the crowd thinned, and made surreptitious reports to Veronica as she'd asked back in the early spring. She seemed interested and appreciative, but somehow just…off. She was like an iceberg: all glorious, shiny surface, but you had no idea how dangerous underneath.

"So that's about it, Veronica. Nothing much to tell this week. Oh, you know that new guy, Serge? Joined up last month? He said he could score some Dianabol. Had to go back to his old contacts at Planet Gym to get 'em, but there was some problem with him not being allowed on the premises."

"Thank you, Victor. I appreciate your diligence. You'll let me know if you ever find out who the big guy is, won't you?" Her eyes were big and round, all innocent and interested. She said "big guy" funny, though, with a weird little smile.

"Do you, maybe, think that the big guy doesn't really exist?" He watched her closely. She toyed with a sleek designer pen.

"Perhaps." Her lips curved in that funny smile again. She shook back her gorgeous chestnut mane and looked at her watch. "Like Santa Claus, maybe." It seemed a very odd comparison to Victor.

"Okey-dokey, then. See you later." Victor blew out a big breath. He always hated reporting to his superior. At least she hadn't —

"Oh, and Victor?"

Framed in the doorway, Victor froze at the sound of her voice.

"About that night…"

He hoped against hope she was going to apologize, knowing it just wasn't going to happen.

"I have a long, long memory." Her beautiful face was cold, like marble, like a tombstone, "And one day, you'll pay. I'm just biding my time until I find out what's really dear to you." He jumped, startled, as she unexpectedly clanked a bangled hand down on the blond wood. "And I'll hurt you as you hurt me!"

"Veronica, it's not like we —"

She held up her hand, the palm reddened from whacking the desk. A warm smile made an appearance, like the sun rising over an ice-capped mountain, "And I look forward to your next report." She held his gaze a long moment, then turned her attention back to the tidy piles of paper on her desk. Dismissed!

Victor shivered and left without speaking another word, his inner voice screaming, *you put the polar in bi-polar, bitch!*

Strangely, the gym's sound system was playing "Hot, Hot, Hot." And usually Victor liked reggae.

Not long after that, the new guy, Serge, found himself banned from yet another gym.

"Hey, Victor!" Phil hollered from his office behind the reception counter. Victor, just a few feet away, heard him annoyingly well.

"What?" Victor was tempted to holler right back.

Phil emerged from his office, saying. "Gus just called and said he'd be late, maybe not get here till seven."

"So?"

"He's got a couple of new members coming at five thirty. You gotta stay and cover for him."

Victor bristled at Phil's attitude — just assuming Victor had nothing better to do than hang around the gym. "Can't tonight, Phil. I've got a date with the cable guy. And I am not rescheduling!"

"Don't care about your love life, Victor. Just stay the extra half hour to give the new guys a quick run-through."

Victor glared rather pointlessly. Phil's half-hour was more like two hours, 'cause dear old Victor could be counted on to give the new guys the full treatment. After all, they would have paid their membership fees in good faith; not their fault some minimum-wage musclehead couldn't tell time. Not Victor's fault either. The only thing keeping him from stalking out then and there was the slightly pleading tone in Phil's voice — well, more like wheedling, actually. That and the fact that Victor really needed to keep this job — needed to stay working at this gym.

"Can't you cover, Phil? You have to be here anyway." Victor could whine with the best of them. "You know how hard it is to get an appointment with the cable company." Nothing like a local monopoly to put an end to customer service.

"Me?" Phil was incredulous. "What do I know from working out?" Which just confirmed what Victor had suspected for a while. "I just run the business side of the business. You have to stay. You'll get overtime."

Oh, great. Another person who thought Victor could be bought. What? Did he have RENT BOY written on his forehead? Or more likely CHEAP'N'EASY. Well, if the latter, he had to admit it was probably in his own handwriting.

Doug appeared in the doorway of Phil's office. "I could go to your apartment and await the cable serviceperson."

Victor hadn't been aware that his friend was working in the manager's office. Doug had started bookkeeping part-time for Veronica earlier in the month in return for a heavily discounted membership. Victor hadn't managed to jibe schedules with Doug in a week or so — Doug had a major accounting assignment, plus the bookkeeping for Orr's. Victor himself had had a number of other commitments that ate up his free time. Victor took a second to appraise his trainee's progress in the fitness areas.

"Victor."

Doug certainly looked good in the black tennis shorts and gray tank Victor had forced him to buy on another shopping expedition.

"Victor."

Doug appeared to have dropped about half the thirty extra pounds he'd been carrying.

"Victor!"

And he'd really toned up. And even gotten a bit of a tan on his formerly pale skin. He'd agreed to go running in a tank top after Victor helpfully compared him to a slug's underbelly.

"Victor!"

Earth to Victor. Stop drooling, he's supposed to be your friend. Your respect-my-goddamn-straightness friend.

"If that's alright with you, of course."

"Sure, Victor, Doug'll do it. Make everybody happy. Me, you, Gus's 5:30s." Phil's smug smile morphed into a suspicious frown. "You don't think you're going to get paid for it, do you, Doug?"

Defensively Victor answered for Doug, "Why would he think that, Phil? He's not getting paid anything now!" He felt a bit guilty. Should he offer his overtime pay to Doug? Half?

Victor was still mad about the raw deal Doug was getting on the bookkeeping for a discounted membership thing. After Doug had done the deal without Victor's knowledge, Victor had taken him aside and not-so-quietly informed him nobody ever paid full price for a membership, so essentially Veronica was getting a certified accountant to do her books for nothing. Doug, however, had stated that he intended to honor his commitment. Of course he did.

Now Doug was answering Phil's question: "No. No. Of course not. I'll meet the cable installer. I'd consider it a gesture of friendship."

Trust Doug to bail him out. "Thanks, Doug. I owe you one. And Phil — he owes us both one. Or is that two? Anyway, you owe us, right, Phil?"

Suddenly, elsewhere was somewhere Phil had to be. Urgently. He returned to his office and his paperwork.

"What time do you anticipate the installer's arrival?"

"You know the cable guys." Victor rolled his eyes. Surprisingly, Doug did too. "The best they'll offer is sometime between six and nine o'clock. And they're usually late. They should know what the problem is, but just in case, tell 'em the frigging cable isn't working and to fix it! They're not even giving me a break on my cable bill for the week and a half it's been out. And get them to install an extra jack in the bedroom. I would have done the splitter thing myself, but I don't want a whole long bunch of cable running 'round the apartment. They got the right tools."

Victor extracted a key ring from the cuff of his sock — no pockets in spandex — and handed the jangling keys to Doug. "You know where to park and all, right?"

"Oh, I couldn't take your car, Victor. I'll take the streetcar."

"Take the car, Doug. You're doing me a favor, after all. And by *me* I mean *Phil*. And Gus!" Victor glared at Phil's doorway. "The least I can do is take public transit myself."

"But —"

"Take the car, Doug."

"I —"

"Take the car, Doug."

"You —"

"Take the car, Doug."

Doug nodded, accepting the keys. Victor was finally learning how to handle his overly courteous friend.

Victor felt eyes on him and turned to see Veronica posed in the doorway of her office, coolly observing their exchange. Something about her stance said *raptor* to Victor, and not in the basketball sense of the word. He felt like prey for a second. A frisson of unease tickled his spine.

It seemed like a good moment to reinforce the *sorry, I'm exclusively gay* line he'd given her that night at her place, so he told Doug louder than necessary, "I'll see you at home around eight o'clock. We'll order in and watch a movie or...whatever." He gave a flirty little lilt to *whatever*, just for effect. "You know your way around my apartment by now — just make yourself at home — put on a movie or something since the goddamn cable isn't working!" God, that pissed him off.

"Thank you, Victor. I'll take good care of your Ram and your apartment."

"My what? Oh. That's Goat, Doug. Goat." He shuddered at the idea of being seen driving a decidedly uncool Dodge Ram.

Two guys entered the gym's reception area: early thirties, attractive, one lanky and one short. The short guy stepped uncertainly up to the counter. "Hi. I called earlier. I'm to ask for Gus."

Phil reemerged from his office and gestured toward Victor with his knockoff Mont Blanc pen. "Nice to see you again, guys. Unfortunately —"

"Hi, I'm Victor, and I'll be your Gus for the evening." The new members looked confusedly from Victor to Phil, who merely nodded.

"See you at home, Doug." Victor peered nervously in the boss-lady's direction. She leaned against the doorframe, crossed arms wrinkling the dark red linen of her well-cut suit.

Shaking off the superstitious feeling of being cursed, Victor grabbed the omnipresent clipboard like a shield, warding off Veronica's evil eye.

"Come with me —" A glance at the paperwork. "Jed?" The short guy nodded. "And Karl. Have I got a gym to show you." He headed toward the stairs, the bewildered Jed and Karl trailing behind. "So, you want to be flattered or hear it straight up?"

⚹ ⚹ ⚹

Victor juggled two oily bags of takeout, his gym stuff and a couple of large bottles of soda pop, nearly losing the contents of one of the bags as he struggled up the stairs to his floor. He practically ran down the hall trying to maintain equilibrium, and just managed to plunk everything down on the floor in front of his apartment while he searched for his…well, of course. Doug had his keys. "Take the car, Doug." Shit.

He rested against the doorframe a moment, winded by the stairs and juggling act as he hadn't been by a full workout and long day in the gym.

He was just about to knock on his own front door when he heard something that arrested further movement: a guy's voice crooning huskily, but loudly, "Ooo, baby. Give it to me. You've got the biggest dick I've ever seen!" A second voice, obviously male as well: "Yeah. Suck it, now, you animal." Groans and cries and *Oh, baby*s drifted softly through the cheap wood of the apartment door. Holy shit! Was Doug getting down with the cable guy? In my apartment? Hell, it sounded like a bad movie. A really bad porn movie. A bad gay porn movie…

Victor felt there was something he wasn't getting here. It certainly did sound like porn… *Wait a minute!* He snapped mental fingers. Neither voice sounded like Doug, although Victor had never had the opportunity to hear what a horny Doug sounded like…much as he'd like to. Much as he'd fantasized…

Victor unguttered his mind and paid attention to the voices leaking out into the hallway. The dialogue sounded familiar, not that he'd paid that much attention to dialogue — like something he'd heard recently. As recently as last night in fact. Oh, God. This was funny. Too funny. Doug was watching gay porn: the video that Victor had left in the VCR last night after his little solo flight to orgasmland!

Victor listened a few moments more, wondering if he should just go away for a while and let Doug watch in peace, but the food would get cold, the cable guy would probably interrupt anyway, and besides, this was just too good to walk away from. The Cheshire Cat had nothing on Victor as he headed back down the stairs to the landing below. He reached behind the radiator, drawing out dust, cobwebs and one large, pissed-off spider, as well as the extra key he'd hidden there for emergencies when he'd first moved into the building.

He rushed back to his apartment, listened a moment longer. "Fuck me harder!" seemed to be the theme of the current scene — and, as quietly as possible, opened the door.

Doug could sure move fast under the right circumstances; the TV was off by the time Victor finished saying, "Hi, Doug. What're you watching?" But the bulge in Doug's track pants remained unaffected by the TV's off switch.

Doug looked so distressed Victor decided to cut him some slack, and went to retrieve the stranded parcels from the hallway. He piled the takeout on the kitchen counter where the leaking hot and sour soup could do little damage, dropped his gym stuff in the hall closet, and came over to stand behind the couch where sat the beet-red and slightly panting Doug.

Doug started wildly when Victor placed his hands on Doug's shoulders and squeezed lightly. He relaxed back into Victor's touch a bit as Victor remarked how tense he was and began massaging his neck, traps, delts, commenting from a professional point of view on Doug's muscle development and overall tone. "Looking good there, Doug." Thumbs ground into knotted traps. "All that sweat is starting to pay off, making you hard." Victor gripped Doug's shoulders tightly as he felt his guest start to pull away. "Your muscles, Doug. Jeez. What did you think I meant?" Victor's evil twin was so enjoying this.

He worked the muscles around what he figured were the guy-safe areas of Doug's body, straying further down his arms and chest each time, pushing the envelope of what he guessed Doug would allow. Doug leaned back into his touch, his breathing more and more ragged. "Lean forward," Victor ordered, bowing gracelessly over the couch's back to reach more of Doug's broad back and shoulders. Doug began to moan with the pressure on such sensitive spots. Victor's own fatigued muscles complained at the awkward stretch and angle, so, without stopping his seductive massage, he eased himself around the side of the sofa and squeezed into the space between Doug and the armrest. Doug was practically purring under his touch. Figuring it was time to really test the waters, Victor headed gradually outward from Doug's shoulder blades, moving under his arms, careful not to tickle as he worked his way across to Doug's chest. The unresisting Doug actually moved his arms a bit out from his sides to accommodate Victor's journey.

Victor thought it pretty obvious that they'd moved from friendly backrub into the heady realm of foreplay. His own hard-on jabbed painfully at his zipper; his breathing roughened as he massaged Doug's hard pecs, concentrating on stimulating his nipples in a surreptitious manner they could both pretend was still a friendly massage. Doug groaned and let his head fall back on Victor's shoulder, and Victor nuzzled whatever part of the man he could reach. Nobody could pretend this was anything but foreplay now.

The loud knocking caused them to jump away from each other in surprise.

"Oh, shit!"

"Oh, dear!"

"Cable Company," came loudly from the hallway.

Victor left the dazed Doug on the couch and, adjusting himself harshly, ushered in a pair of workers wearing jeans and formerly white polo shirts featuring the company's logo over their hearts.

"Trainee," explained the cable guy, hooking thumb over shoulder at the accompanying cable girl. "What's the problem?"

Without waiting for an answer, the cable guy grabbed the TV remote from the coffee table and hit the *On* button. Instantly the still-running VCR treated them to a Technicolor fuck-fest featuring two men, their black and white skins in sharp contrast as groans and the slap of damp flesh provided the mortifying soundtrack, nearly drowning out a really cheesy version of "Knock Three Times" that Tony Orlando was probably unaware of.

Victor lunged for the remote, practically tackling the serviceman to get control of the control. Doug bypassed the literal power struggle and simply hit the off switch on the face of the TV. He then ejected the video, turned off the VCR, inserted the tape into its plain cardboard case, and handed it to Victor.

"You said watch a movie." His voice was steady, but his hands were shaking. "So I watched a movie." He turned and wove his way with great care around furniture and people to the dining alcove, where he sat down heavily in one of the straight-backed chairs.

Victor handed the remote back to the cable guy and hid in the kitchen, fussing with their cooling dinner, although he wasn't hungry at this point and neither, he guessed, was Doug.

"Fucking fags!" The cable guy's snarl was audible, despite the pretence at whispering, followed by this gem of logic: "No wonder the cable don't work."

"Shut up, Travis! They're people too, you know." Damned by faint praise, Victor thought, hardly inspired by the trainee's sorry defense.

"Victor," Doug said, whisper-soft. Victor emerged from the kitchen, drying his hands on a souvenir of Niagara Falls dishtowel. Doug lifted his eyes to meet Victor's for just a moment. Victor's heart soared. Perhaps he'd be forgiven his latest transgression. "Don't forget about the extra jack in the bedroom," Doug said, then left the apartment.

Victor figured he'd be eating cold Chinese for a week. Alone.

HE SHALL BE LEVON

In a repeat of their previous awkward morning-after, there was some training, some talking and some takeout. Mostly they fell all over themselves trying to take the blame and apologize. After a few days everything was cool between them again, and they went back to being just buddies. After all, nothing had really happened, right? Just a guy getting a bit of a rubdown from his best friend and personal trainer.

Time passed. Doug lost five more pounds, which Victor insisted represented a greater loss since muscle was heavier than fat. "And you're building muscle," Victor had elaborated. Nelly suggested they settle the argument with the fat calipers. But Victor claimed they were a bunch of bullshit that could be made to say any damned old thing necessary to convince people they needed to join the gym, then show them they were making progress whether they were or not. Victor insisted that something about being weighed under water was the only way to determine actual body fat percentages, but he couldn't quite recall the details of the article he'd read. Thus the argument stood, but the bottom line was that if Doug had been attractive when he'd first joined the gym, several months of solid workouts under his belt — quite literally! — had made him truly devastating. Everybody wanted him and gay men were rarely known for their shyness.

Victor had actually caught Doug playing up their relationship in order to get out of the awkwardness of being repeatedly hit on. Victor sighed and played along. He might not be getting any play at Orr's but it was his workplace, after all, so he really shouldn't mix cruising with business. Besides, as Doug's friend, pretending to be his boyfriend was the least he could do. He didn't really want anyone else, anyway. His pretend relationship with Doug was turning out to be the best relationship he'd ever had, including his ex-marriage.

One evening the faux boyfriends were making plans to get together at Victor's place. There was a special on the Discovery Channel about Northern Ontario that featured some First Nations friends of Doug's youth that Doug really wanted to see. Victor was curious about Doug's upbringing and so wanted to see it as well. He found himself unable to relate to anything that didn't involve growing up in a world-class city of two and a half million people.

Doug was tidying up his account books in Phil's office and Victor was finishing his paperwork when Levon and crew stopped at the front desk to get information on a bodybuilding competition taking place later that month. Since Victor was the only staff member around, he helpfully fetched the flyers provided by the contest organizers.

As they were leaving the front desk, Doug emerged from the manager's office and went to lean on the counter near Victor, waiting for him to finish up. Levon, in true charming style, turned back from the stairwell and called, "Don't forget to practice safe sucks, girls!"

Victor shot him a look, but Levon was long gone, master of the hit-and-run barb, as always. Victor mumbled something about *going too far* and *one of these days*. Doug looked at him curiously.

They grabbed pizza this time — it was known as Chicago-style, but Victor said it had never been south of the forty-ninth parallel. And he would know, having been to the Windy City once on a grade 11 field trip. It was really, really good though. The documentary was interesting, although great chunks of it would have to be re-watched later from the tape Victor had made because Doug's explanations, elaborations and anecdotes had masked much of the soundtrack. Still, the scenery had been nice. Plus there'd been moose!

He snapped the little plastic tab off the video case so mistakes couldn't happen and thought again about getting one of the personal video recorder things that recorded right onto a computer hard drive.

Pizza pleasantly digesting, an action flick on the VCR for background noise, the friends relaxed on the sofa, beers in hand.

"Can I ask you something, Victor?"

"If I said no, would you anyway?"

"No. Of course not. I always respect your privacy."

"Okay. No."

There was a lengthy silence, during which they paid cursory attention to the movie. Victor got up twice to use the bathroom, mumbling, "You drink one beer…" Jack-the-dog was let out and back in and out and in, and he hadn't even had a beer.

Three beers each later, Doug took up the question thing again, as Victor had known he would. "Victor. Why can't I ask you a question?"

"Because you asked if you could ask. Next time just ask."

Another silence while Doug appeared to be puzzling this out.

"Ah. Victor?"

"Yes, Doug?"

"Why do you let that young man speak to you like that? I can't imagine you allowing anyone else to treat you in that highly disrespectful manner. Why is it that Levon can persist without reprisal?"

Victor sighed and muted the TV, figuring this would be a lengthy and tricky conversation. "Because I get him. I know what he's going through. Why he's acting out."

"I'm sorry?"

"That's okay. Just don't do it again." Relieved, he turned the sound back up.

"No, Victor. I meant I fail to take your meaning. What is it that you get about him?"

Victor sighed again, and paused the movie altogether. Arnold would just have to wait until this conversation with Doug was over. He dropped his feet from the coffee table to the floor, using the momentum to swing his body around so he was facing Doug across a foot or so of sofa. Doug looked at him expectantly.

"Because." Victor paused meaningfully. "The hardest part of coming out is coming out to yourself."

Doug *ah'*d and nodded in comprehension. Victor waited.

"No. I'm afraid I'm still at a loss. Coming out of what?"

"The closet, Doug. Coming out of the closet."

"I see."

Again Victor waited, watching Doug earnestly.

"No. I don't see. Victor, could you be a little more forthcoming in your explanations, please?"

Oh. The return of snappish Doug. He did not seem to like being in any way out of control.

"He's gay, Doug. Or at least bi."

Now Doug got it, if the expression of surprised comprehension was anything to go by.

"He just doesn't know it yet," Victor concluded.

"Ah. He's gay." Doug repeated. "But he doesn't know it. And you do? Do I have it correctly now?"

Victor nodded with some satisfaction, but sat there expecting more conversation.

"I'm fairly well read, Victor. And since, um, meeting you and, experiencing a bit of your, er, lifestyle, however vicariously" — quick glance at Victor, then back to the knee he was examining — "I've made a point of reading a bit about, um, gay culture." Doug seemed to be having trouble expressing himself. He drew a deep breath and continued. "And I'm under the impression that the entire 'gay-dar' phenomenon" — and here Doug made irritating little finger motions to indicate quotation marks — "is something of a myth. However, if you've a technique —"

"Nah, Nah. Nothing like that." Victor waved a dismissive hand in the air. "He told me."

"He told you he was gay, but he doesn't know it?"

"That's right. Now you're getting it."

Doug sat back, crossing his arms, posture clearly stating *you are not quite right in the head*, and asked Victor to elaborate.

"It's really not my story to tell, so I got to ask you to keep it under your hat. If you wore a hat." Doug nodded. "And you'd probably look good in one. Something with a brim maybe. Okay. Right. Levon." Four beers, despite a hearty helping of pizza, was fucking with Victor's concentration a little.

"One night when I first started working at Orr's, I was on late shift — new guy always gets the crappy shift. Anyway, there was hardly anybody around and I'm doing a security check — you know, walking the place like on patrol, right?" Doug nodded for him to continue. "So I go down to the change room to get something out of my locker, and I hear these snuffling noises coming from one of the bathroom stalls. So I'm concerned, maybe somebody got hurt or something, so I check it out. Stall door's not locked or anything, so I kind of ask if the guy's okay in there. I mean, you can't just go barging into a stall in a men's room that close to the gay ghetto — what I thought was sniffling could have been somebody with allergies getting the blow job of his life. Plus women will sometimes — *Douglas Newkirk. You have been hanging with me for months now. Get over the blushing stuff, will you?*"

Before Doug could launch into some Discovery Channel spiel about involuntary bodily functions, Victor continued. "So I get no answer and I open the door a little and see Levon sitting there on the john, lid closed, all dressed, trying not to let me see his face 'cause he's crying. I ask him if he's hurt and he tells me to fuck off, which I know means he's hurting, just not from any physical-type accident in the gym. So I talk to him for a bit, just rambling on about life and stuff, and finally I get him to come out and wash his face. He feels a little more human after that, I guess, and sits on the bench with me.

"We talk awhile, and turns out there's this boy in their gang — and it's not a real gang-banger-type gang, just a bunch of middle-class, banger-wannabe kids who hang around together — and Levon thought he and this kid were close. He put himself out for this kid, getting him accepted into the group when he first started hanging with them, and he spent a lot of time with the guy: meeting him after school, lending him money, helping with homework, sleeping over at his house." He paused to give emphasis to the last. "So once the boy — Delroy, I think he called him — so once Delroy gets into the group all cozy-like, he drops Levon like a hot yam, and moves up the gang ranks. 'Cause, like, every gang has its social structure —"

"Pack behavior," Doug contributed. "Alpha, beta, chosen females. Although among wolves, it's often the female—"

"Yeah. You get it. Gangs are structured more like royalty, though — little tribes, like. The king, royal advisor, second-in-command, court jester, mascot — roles like that."

"You sound like you've given this some thought."

"I'm a very observant fellow. I like to watch."

Doug looked mildly confused by the statement, but declined to interrupt. Nor did he ask for further clarification on the subject of Victor's watching — after all, Victor recalled, Doug had once accused Victor of watching him.

"So this guy dumping Levon is pretty typical male behavior — use or be used, right? But Levon, he's not reacting in a typical guy way, getting pissed off, dissing the guy, pissing in his Pepsi, whatever. Guys aren't very nice people. Ever notice that, Doug?"

Doug apparently could recognize a rhetorical question given the right circumstances, so Victor continued. "Anyway, Levon is just crushed at getting dumped."

Doug still looked unconvinced.

"Does that sound like regular boyish behavior to you, Doug? Two young boys, so attached, then one leaves and the other just falls apart?" He trailed off.

"And how does his ongoing rudeness and inappropriate behavior toward you fit into your analysis, Dr. Brighton?" Doug's tone was prickly.

"Kid's in denial — big time. He's posturing like a dog, well, dog in that pack-behavior anal…anal…" Before Doug could blush, Victor found the word he was looking for: "…analogy of yours. Puffing up — bristling — to look bigger than he is."

Doug looked pensive for several long minutes, no doubt giving thoughtful consideration to Victor's story. Finally, he looked at Victor. "And this — tears at a friend's betrayal and taunting of the man who witnessed his embarrassing lapse — doesn't seem to you normal adolescent behavior? Instead, this, in your estimation, makes him gay?"

"Or bi. Yeah."

"Even if it were true that he had 'a thing,' albeit in this case unrequited, for young Delroy, as I believe I've said before, one childhood transgression does not a sexual orientation make," Doug said emphatically.

"Yeah." Pause. "Are we still talking 'bout Levon here?" Victor asked softly.

"I might well ask you the same question. Were we ever talking 'bout Levon here?"

Victor ignored the question. "I just want the kid to be happy." His voice rose. "I want him to be the well-adjusted fucking adolescent I never got the chance to be. So if it'll help any, I'll cut the kid some slack — take his bullshit. It won't hurt me, sticks and stones and all that."

"Right." Doug clammed up. Victor switched the movie back on, and they watched in silence as speeding cars chased each other and were shot up with futuristic weapons.

The action-packed movie ended, leaving them feeling exhilarated — yet tired from sitting so long. Victor yawned and stretched, cracking his neck. Doug did the same, and when their stretched-out arms came in contact, both men pulled away quickly.

"You want I should drive you home now, Doug?"

"Thank you, Victor, but I'll, of course, call a…Can I ask you a…No. I'll just ask."

"So ask already."

"You said earlier… Perhaps this isn't the time. I'll be going now."

"Jesus, Doug, just ask the stupid question. God, you sure get on a guy's last nerve."

"Well, Victor. If you put it that way," Doug said sulkily, then collected himself and continued in more sympathetic tones. "You said earlier that you wished Levon could have the well-adjusted adolescence you never had. What did you mean by that?"

"What I actually said was…"

"I know what you said, Victor," Doug cut in sharply. "And really, I've been meaning to speak to you about your language for some time now. However, this is not the time, so please continue; that is, if you feel you would like to answer…well, no. Perhaps I'd better just…" This time he rose to leave, getting halfway up off the couch before Victor grabbed his arm and dragged him back down.

"Hold your horses. Hold your horses. I'll answer the question. What is this, the Spanish incubation?"

"Sometimes I think you do that on purpose, Victor."

"Do what?" Victor asked, giving his best innocent look, the one Yolanda had called "Punk Angel: the Ghost of Sid Vicious Past."

"You want to hear my life story?" Doug nodded. "It'll take awhile. Way longer than Levon's, 'cause I'm way older, of course. I don't think you really want to do this."

"Ah, but I do, Victor. I want to know all there is to know about you."

Victor gazed at him thoughtfully.

"I'm your friend, after all," Doug added hastily, looking away.

Victor went to get them yet more beers, Doug having switched from grapefruit juice somewhere during the Levon conversation. Whoa, four beers over the course of an entire evening. Doug might be able accuse him of corrupting him after all.

"'Kay. Here we go." He leaned back on the couch, feet gracing the coffee table once more, closed his eyes a moment. And began.

"I guess I was about eleven or twelve when I first started jacking off."

"Victor!"

"You want to hear this or not, Doug? 'Cause I already know how it turns out. You're the new guy here who wants to take a ride through the tunnel of Vic. I mean, hear my life story, 's'all."

"You're right, of course, Victor. Please continue. I'm sorry."

"Right. Right. Sorry's good. Now where was I? Right. Jerking off." Daring Doug to interrupt again, he settled back into the cushions once more. "So I'm your typical kid — sneaking a peek at the skin mags at the 7-Eleven, following the other little boys when we get a chance to see little Barbie Scott's days-o'-the-week panties. Snickering and trading dirty jokes when we're alone. Normal little boy stuff.

"Except I find myself also peeking at the other guys in the locker room, in the can. And maybe this is normal, too — just trying to see what the other guy's got, but then the jerking-off thing starts, and I find that in addition to Barbie Ann's underpants, I'm also thinking about her brother Glen and what he looks like changing for gym class. I'm even having dreams — dreams about neighbors and teachers, even frickin' TV characters — guys, girls, old, young — my libido's just all over the place. And let me tell you, this twelve-year-old was freaking the fuck out.

"I was a good Catholic boy, raised in a working-class neighborhood by blue-collar parents — dad was a meat packer and mom was a secretary at the plant once she went back to work. When we were small, she stayed home to look after my brother and me.

"Anyway, they were good parents, but not exactly enlightened, a bit like your grandparents, maybe."

Doug nodded. Acknowledgement? Agreement? Encouragement? Who could tell?

"So I'm freaking. Should I tell my parents? Should I confess to Father O'Reilly? Talk to the guidance counselor? I'm wondering around in a daze for so long it starts affecting my schoolwork. Then bam! I walk into this dance class my parents enrolled me in. Yeah, yeah. I was always tripping over my own feet and my parents thought maybe it would make me graceful or something. Anyway… Where was I? Right. Right. And wham! There's this girl! The most beautiful girl I'd ever seen. I never felt anything like it — like getting struck by lightning: no, an atom bomb. An Adam bomb and she's my Eve. And that's okay. That's good. That's normal. I hang onto that for dear life. For most of my goddamn life.

"And it isn't easy. My parents don't like her 'cause she comes from money. 'Stick with your own', they say. 'She's just toying with you'. And she's not Catholic. Not from the neighborhood. Too full of herself. And that's just on my end. Her parents are giving her all the same grief in reverse: he's too wild. No class. Not Anglican — whatever difference that makes; ten years married and I still don't know. All this to a couple of kids. But no matter what, or maybe because of it, we clung to each other, like lifelines. Like life itself.

"'Course we were just friends when we met — fifteen years old, although we were seventeen before we actually 'did it'. Guess we were late bloomers compared with you and hockey boy." Doug gasped, but Victor continued. He had some vague plan to gently tease his friend about the childhood affair until gradually he became desensitized to the memory.

"Slowly, we started being together. She let me hold her hand, then kiss her, then…more." At Doug's look, uncomfortable and disapproving at the same time, he hastily amended the detailed description he'd meant to give. "Like I said, we were seventeen before we actually went all the way.

"After the grocery store robbery incident?" Doug asked.

"Yeah. Right. That." Victor looked away. Sometimes it all seemed so long ago that it was more like a memory of something that had happened to someone else. Sometimes it seemed like last year.

"For years, we went steady — going around, it was called in those days — for months at a time, then we'd fight or let our parents come between us and break up for a while. We'd lose track of when we were together and when we weren't. It was hard to tell, 'cause we'd have sex with each other even during the broken-up times. Sometimes we'd go out with other people. I think she'd meet someone she felt like sleeping with, dump me for the duration of the fling, then haul me back in when she got bored of him and ready to spend time with good ol' Victor again. I usually waited for her, but not always. This went on for years.

"I might not have gone to college without her influence. She encouraged me when I didn't think I was very smart. This college thing my parents approved of, so for once they were smiling on Yolanda. She enrolled in social work studies or something like that. Me, I wanted to teach phys ed, so I took kinesiology. Yeah. I know, pretty ambitious, but I was pretty good in math and science, and I was doing okay there in first year, but maybe I wouldn't have made the cut, I don't know, and I never got the chance to find out."

"What happened, Victor?"

"This is the part that gets hard for me; the bear I have to cross. Lemme tell it and don't interrupt. Okay?"

Doug opened his mouth to comment, then closed it without speaking and simply nodded again.

"See, I was still having all these feelings, attractions, sexual attractions toward guys, but every time I felt really drawn toward a particular guy, I just turned all my attention back on Yolanda. That way I could sub…sublimate my feelings toward guys and pretend to the whole world, myself included, that I was straight, straight, straight. After all, I had the perfect girl, didn't I?

"But sometimes when we were broken up I'd meet somebody, and when I went to college, it was the late '80s and everybody was experimenting and getting caught up in politically correct causes. There actually seemed to be some reverse prejudice going on — if you were black or gay you were automatically cool. Everybody wanted to be your friend. So now it's like a balloon getting ready to pop."

Doug quirked one eyebrow, which Victor took to mean *Lucy, you got some 'splaining to do* — only in Canadian instead of Cuban, eh.

"You know, a balloon keeps its shit together because it has equal pressure on the outside and the inside."

Doug nodded. Victor thought he was starting to look like one of those little nodding dogs in the back of cars. A really good-looking little nodding dog. Victor was getting really tired and the beer wasn't helping him keep his thoughts on the straight and narrow — especially the straight.

"So the pressure to go out and do something with these urges was still strong from the inside, but the pressure to keep it under wraps, keep a lid on it, was weakening. So, the balloon's getting ready to burst. See?"

Apparently Doug saw.

"So one time early in the spring of our first year, just after exams I think it was, we break up. Again. And a few days later, I get dragged by friends to this party, then to a bar, then to an after-hours club, and I get cruised by this guy — a good looking older guy named Frank. Least that's what he said his name was. And now that I think about it, I bet he was younger than I am now, but at the time, he seemed so mature and sophisticated. I let him take me home. I let him... anything he wanted."

He paused a long time, forgetting his guest, his apartment, his life, just... remembering. Finally he returned to himself, grinning sheepishly at Doug and wondering how likely it was that his overly observant friend wouldn't notice the growing lump in his track pants. He shifted a bit on the couch.

"It was, um, pretty amazing. I know you can't even imagine it, but it was great. We did it so many times that night. And then I never saw him again. I couldn't have found the apartment again if I tried — matter of fact, I did try. Took me awhile to realize Frank must have intentionally given me a wrong phone number.

"So here's me having discovered the greatest new thing ever — lots of wild sex with sexy strangers without any commitments or complications. After all the years and all the shit Yolanda and I put each other through, it was just great. And for a few short weeks, I made the best of it. I put the *fruit* in forbidden fruit." He grinned evilly.

"You're lucky you didn't catch anything," Doug interjected with a hint of a question in his voice.

"Yeah. Damn lucky. It was early on in the whole AIDS thing, and so sometimes I used a rubber and sometimes I didn't. It was hard to get my head around using a condom when there was no chance the other guy was going to get pregnant. But I'm clean, just in case you were wondering." He leered at Doug, who blushed, maybe because he had been wondering. Victor could hope, couldn't he?

"So Yolanda and me had been broken up a couple of months. We'd still get together pretty often, sometimes even screw — nobody can make her come like I can."

"Victor!"

"Sorry, Doug, but it's true — you spend years studying something, practicing every chance you get, you get pretty good at it. I'm surprised she doesn't still call me sometimes." Victor made some karate-chop moves with his hands, then did something pretty athletic with his tongue: "*Ai-ya!* I have a black belt in cunnilingus." He waved his karate hands again and grinned. Doug sighed and examined the ceiling. He was blushing pretty much continuously now. Victor figured literal-minded Doug wasn't going to put in an appearance here and ask if there really was such a field of study among the ancient Oriental arts. Victor sometimes wondered if Doug did that on purpose, the naïve-literal thing. Kind of like Victor's own fucking with words and phrases thing. God, he'd like to fuck with…never mind.

"Anyway," he continued. "This time it's different. She wants to get back together, and I can't imagine why I would want to do that. I love her and all, but hey, I'm young, working my ass off in college, plus a part-time job, and suddenly I've got this whole new sex thing going on. I'm not just fucking men — sorry, Doug — but women were pretty easy back in those mostly-pre-AIDS days too. I'm re-defining bisexuality on a daily basis — I figure it's the ultimate bi-partisan statement the day I bed a hardcore lesbian. And her girlfriend. And *her* boyfriend." He waggled his eyebrows, then asked, "What?" defensively at Doug's look.

"But Yolanda's after me again and she's all teary-eyed and we end up in bed, as per usual, and wham! Lightning strikes again. She's pregnant. And she says it's mine. She hasn't been with anyone but me during the likely timeframe…yadda yadda.

"So now I'm freaking out for a whole new reason. I'm going to be a daddy. I don't even think for a moment about anything else. I tell my parents and they're way past pissed. I've got this really good summer job at a local garage working as an apprentice mechanic: pays big-man salary, none of your student training-wage crap. So I tell the boss I'm staying on, marry Yolanda quick at a Protestant church, and figure I've got the whole package ready to go. It's ironic, though, that just when I finally come to grips with my attraction to men, I end up with the bullet-proof cover — a wife and family."

"But you're not a mechanic now, though," Doug said, pretty much missing the entire point of the story. Victor figured his friend had focused on the one thing he was comfortable with about the whole tale.

"Nah. My grease-monkey days are behind me. Thought I'd pursue something else for a while. Something where I didn't come home filthy every night. Or at least not as often. And didn't I say something about not interrupting?" He mock-glared.

"Sorry, Victor. Please continue." Doug made a sweeping gesture that would have done a respectable maître d' proud.

Victor harrumphed. "Anyway. Now, to say that her family was pissed would be a major understatement. They never even came to the wedding. Their golden girl marrying the poor kid from the wrong side of the tracks — what was she thinking? But she loved me, and we were living together in a little one-bedroom walkup." He glanced around his present apartment. "Pretty much like this one, actually. And we were fucking day and night. And for once we didn't have to worry about birth control. It was great.

"Then one day after we'd only been married a couple of weeks, I come home and she's lying on the ratty old couch her parents had given us from their cottage, this huge concession to our marriage, and she's pale and her eyes are puffy and she says she's lost the baby. I blame myself — I think we had too much sex or something. Later I read that couldn't be it.

"Her parents felt that since the baby had been the reason for the marriage, then no baby should mean no marriage. Stone cold logic, right? But Yolanda and I were sticking together. I planned to put her through college, although when she changed her major to law, Daddy the big mucky-muck lawyer suddenly started coughing up bucks for tuition and books and living expenses. Her original plan was to practice public law, be a Crown attorney or something — what the American TV shows call a Public Defender or States Attorney. Anyway, he sucked her into his high-powered law firm and now she runs the downtown office. Maurice works there. That's how I met him and Johnnie in the first place. Believe it or not, Yolanda and I used to double-date with them a fair amount."

Doug had a funny look on his face; dare Victor hope he was jealous? Probably not, probably still embarrassed about the hockey asshole thing. He cast around a bit for the thread of his story, picking it up where he'd left off.

"Anyway, Yolanda, she was all work, work, work, first at law school and then later running the firm. I was lonely because I didn't have many friends, and so I started hinting that she should get pregnant again. Hell, I never hint, you know that," Victor grinned, but continued quickly, afraid he'd strayed across the invisible line they'd drawn on the couch between them. "I started putting the pressure on.

"And she fought me on it big time, but finally said she'd try. And we did try — and nothing. Eventually we went to a doctor together — a gynecologist. Going together is one of those things married couples do," he explained as Doug's previously red face turned pale, pale, pale.

"And after the exam, he called us in and explained that there might be some difficulty getting pregnant because of the scarring from the previous abortion. Apparently, that guy had been a butcher and infection had set in."

Victor's eyes burned as he stared at Doug's knee. The silence became awkward, and Doug finally asked, "The abortion could have been from a previous occasion, could it not?"

"Nah. She gave the doctor all the details, including dates — pretty much matched up with our wedding."

"Perhaps it was a matter of timing. She wanted to have your baby and then changed her mind," Doug offered lamely, fiddling with the scar in his eyebrow.

Victor laughed, a rough and ugly sound. "Oh, no. It gets worse." He wiped one eye on his sleeve before continuing. "At that same doctor appointment where Yolanda's telling him about her hatchet job, he reads this report on me he just got back from the urologist and tells us it's amazing we got pregnant at all back then. Seems my sperm count is about as low as a guy can have and not be singing soprano."

"Victor. Your sperm count has nothing to do with —"

"I know. I know. I was speaking metaphysically."

"Meta...Never mind. Carry on with your tale, Victor.

"So the baby probably wasn't mine in the first place, and anyway she got rid of it. What I never got was why she bothered to marry me if she didn't plan to keep the baby. I never got up the nerve to ask. I didn't want to know. Still don't."

"Perhaps she suspected the baby had been fathered by someone else and didn't feel she could ask you to raise another man's child."

"How would I have known — unless it was black or Chinese or something? Oh Christ! I can't believe I never thought of that before. Talk about denial. Well, shit. Maybe I wasn't the only one out sowing my wild rice with forbidden fruit back then. But still, why not just have the abortion and carry on? Why marry me?"

"Perhaps she loved you, Victor. You're very easy to love." Doug spoke in hushed tones, then shook himself like a wet dog and looked away.

"Thanks, Doug. You're making me feel a bit better about all this." He grinned ruefully at his friend.

"But anyway, the entire point of this long story" — he glanced at the VCR, which still read *12:00, 12:00, 12:00*; he felt it to be around one o'clock in the morning — "was to explain to you why I cut Levon slack. Does it make sense to you now?"

Doug pondered, starting several different replies: "Yes," then, "No," then, "Perhaps," before settling on, "I believe I'll need to sleep on it, Victor."

"Well, you can do it on the couch now, 'cause it's way too late for me to be driving your ass home. You want first dibs on the bathroom?" he asked and began pulling cushions off the sofa bed right over Doug's attempts at protest.

Morning. Awake. Sort of. Voices coming from the other room. What the fuck? Victor groaned, knowing his gun was hidden in the hall closet, the bullets in the kitchen drawer near the spoons. He groaned again and dropped his fuzzy head into his hands. Then his sleep-fogged brain sorted out the voices of Doug, Johnnie, and Maurice. Right. Right. Doug had slept over last night — on the couch.

Not caring that he wore only boxer briefs, he staggered past the guys, waving dismissively at their cheerful greetings and Doug's apology for waking him. He headed for the bathroom to try to take care of his morning piss-on, not relishing the challenging task of trying to aim downward when his dick was pointing up. Fuck it, he thought, stripping off his shorts, everybody pisses in the shower. He climbed in.

After his shower, he felt a little more like himself, and he went to find out why he was being bombarded with early morning visitors. And coffee. Must have coffee.

Conversation turned his way as he entered. "Nice skirt, Brighton," Johnnie commented acerbically.

Victor glanced down at the gaily colored sarong he used as a summer bathrobe. "Fuck you, Bauerman." He swiped Doug's orange juice and downed the contents in one long draught. Coffee next. He found his favorite mug next to the fragrant coffeemaker, a pile of sugar staring back up at him from the bottom of the cup that looked to be exactly his preferred two teaspoons full.

"Thanks, Doug." He joined the others at his faux-pine table and identified the great aromas he'd been sniffing as muffins and Danish. "You guys bring this?" It was barely identifiable as speech, said through a mouthful of sticky bun.

"Yes, oh gracious host." Johnnie's broad grin belied his sarcasm. "The sticky buns that you are currently devouring like some sort of carrion bird were already here, though. Guess Doug's taken the time and trouble to memorize all your special little likes and dislikes." He practically cooed the latter.

The clock radio in Victor's room erupted, making the musical suggestion that they give 'em something to talk about. Victor was sorely tempted. He rather enjoyed the whole pretend boyfriend thing they had done at the gym to discourage Veronica as well as the guys who hit on Doug. He briefly considered stringing Maurice and Johnnie along. But, Maurice didn't deserve it and Johnnie, well, he'd probably get on his cell phone and broadcast it before they could tell him they were only kidding.

He brought his coffee cup to his lips again, swallowed loudly and answered Johnnie's unasked question. "Couch, guys. Doug slept on the couch. Sorry to disappoint you, but Doug's still straight."

Johnnie did indeed seem disappointed; no new gossip to spread around, Victor figured.

"Well, keep at it, Victor. Eventually you'll bring this gorgeous man over to the *lite* side." Grabbing up his almost empty mug, Johnnie fit it over his mouth and started to make loud, labored breathing sounds, followed by, "Luke, I am your lover," in stentorian tones. Johnnie did a mean James Earl Jones — for a white boy.

There was a moderate amount of chuckling in response to this display. Even Doug-the-pop-culturally-impaired must have seen some of the *Star Wars* films.

"Now look what you've done," Maurice admonished his partner in motherish tones. The cup-cum-Darth Vader-mask hadn't been quite empty, and coffee dribbled down the dapper man's shirt and landed on Victor's tabletop. "Where are the napkins, Victor?"

"Top drawer of the sideboard behind you. No wait! I'll get th —" Too late. Johnnie was displaying a pair of gleaming steel handcuffs, pinched between finger and thumb as if they might be unclean. "Do I want to know where these have been, Victor Brighton?"

It's too early for this, Victor thought, gripping his coffee cup like a life preserver.

Thankfully, the long-suffering Maurice saved him. "It's none of our business, John. And besides, we have much nicer ones at home. Fur-lined."

The search for napkins was renewed as Doug contributed his current mouthful of orange juice to the spreading puddle on the table.

The mess was cleaned up and breakfast finished before Maurice remembered why they'd dropped by in the first place. Doug was stacking dishes in the kitchen when Maurice said, "A bunch of my colleagues at Summerwood and Summerwood are throwing me a surprise fortieth birthday party. It's at The Zone next Friday night after work. They've conspired with Johnnie to invite everyone I've ever met. It'll be the bash from hell: lawyers, clients, and half the fags and dykes in the city. And these are not mutually exclusive categories, mind you. Plus my brother Henri is going to be there." Maurice shuddered. Johnnie nodded knowingly. "Please come and bring Doug so there'll be at least two friendly faces there."

"You'll come, won't you?" Maurice called out to Doug in the kitchen.

"Thank you for the invitation, but I'm sure Victor will want to attend this function without me. I'm not much for social affairs. I'm sure he has no end of suitable...escorts for this sort of soirée."

"Ah. But that's that point. It'll just kill Yolanda. You being gorgeous and all." Johnnie took over the conversation. "And yes, Doug, that's a good thing. The killing Yolanda part. And the gorgeous part." He refilled his cup.

Laughing, holding up damp hands in surrender, Doug agreed to discuss it further with Victor. They moved on to other important topics. With Johnnie firmly in control of the conversation, it was mostly about who was doing whom and the semi-annual two-for-one sale at the Bay.

The night of Maurice's "surprise" party, Doug strode down the path from his apartment building, heading for the passenger side of Victor's GTO. He strutted his stuff and did his thang and looked about as cool as a disco king, which would have been fine if it was still 1977. Victor called to him, and Doug moved to stand by the driver's open window instead. He leaned down to Victor's eye level, propping his now-muscular forearms on the window frame, forearms that were bare because Doug had shoved his jacket and shirt sleeves up to his elbows à la disco inferno. Only a few centimeters separated the two men.

"Uh, Doug, you didn't have to wear a suit. It's not that kind of place." Victor eyed the out-of-style three-piece pinstripe warily.

By now, Victor had spent enough time with Doug to have seen him tired, sweaty, sick, upset. None of it had prepared him for Doug looking unattractive. The suit was ill fitting, dated and sloppy. He suddenly got a picture of what fat-Doug must have looked like.

"Oh. But it's a party, Victor — in honor of Maurice's fortieth birthday. Shouldn't you be dressed a little less...casually?" Judgmental? Doug? Surely not, Victor's bitter half sarcasmed.

"Nah. It's at The Zone — totally cas'. Anything goes." He failed to mention that since half the people would be coming straight from the office, they'd probably be in suits as well — with ties and wedding bands stashed safely out of sight. God, he hated amateurs. "It's just that I can't stand suits myself. Feel trapped. Constricted. Don't do bondage well either." He leered evilly.

"And you would know this because...? Never mind. I do not want to know." Doug looked a little uncomfortable, but he didn't blush. Victor figured all his teasing was starting to desensitize his friend a bit. Good.

"Anyway, go change. If you have to be stuck in a loud, smoky bar for the entire night, you want to be comfortable, right?"

"All right, Victor. If you insist. What do you suggest I wear then, if not a suit?"

"Go don ye now your not-gay apparel. Do that lumberjack thing. Looks good on ya."

"Oh. High heels, suspendies and a bra?"

Vertebrae popping like gunfire, Victor executed an Olympic double take.

"'I cut down trees. I wear high heels, suspendies and a bra,'" Doug sang in a respectable tenor.

Victor sputtered wildly, but no actual words emerged.

"One would have to be quite dead to have grown up in the seventies without some exposure to Monty Python. I didn't live in the outback, Victor. I did my commerce degree at Lakehead University in the thriving metropolis of Thunder Bay." Doug appeared to be trying for indignant, but a grin kept sneaking through. "Besides, I'm rather fond of the chorus of singing Mounties. It really offended my father."

Still recovering from the uncharacteristic zinger, Victor stammered, "Just when I think I've got you figured, there you go surprising me again." Victor gazed at him fondly. "I meant jeans and T-shirt or one of your plethora of plaid shirts." Victor grinned back at Doug's delighted smile. If vocabulary turned the man on, he could buy a word-a-day calendar. "But hey, whatever don't get you arrested, my friend."

"I'll be right back. Or would you like to come in while I change?" Doug's residual grin almost turned the statement from innocent good manners into…something else.

If it had been anyone other than Doug, Victor would have figured it as an invitation that would probably result in clothing being removed, but not hurriedly replaced, and totally missing the party. He licked his lips. Doug was standing upright by the car now, his torso framed in the car window, tits to thighs.

The working out was doing wonders — you could tell, even in that nasty old suit. Oops, Doug was waiting for a response, "Nah. I'll wait here." Victor hadn't forgotten the "other end of the couch" comment from a few months back. Or the distressing cable incident. He'd resolved to keep his hands to himself. It was the right thing to do.

A few minutes later, Doug reappeared, having changed into something more suitable than a suit. Victor hid a grin as Doug climbed into the passenger seat — attired in faded, slightly baggy jeans with one knee missing and a tight black T-shirt. The newly birthed Victor clone stared straight ahead, arms crossed defensively across his chest.

"I'm not changing again, Victor. This is the best I can do."

"No. It's fine. You look good. Really. Where'd you get those jeans? I've never seen them before." Victor was glad he had chosen tight black jeans and a gray T-shirt for the evening — should cut down on the separated-at-birth, two-for-one-sale comments that would have resulted from identical post-punk outfits.

"I just bought them. I thought I'd...as you've said on more than one occasion...move into this millennium." Doug placed one hand over his bare knee like a Victorian lady hiding naked, sinful flesh.

Victor stared at Doug a while longer, getting lost in his head for a bit.

"Um. Victor. You're ogling me."

"No, I'm, not Doug. I'm merely assessing your fitness progress."

"Ogling."

"Appraising."

"Ogling."

"Appreciating."

"Ogling."

"Ogling." Busted. Eye-fucking in the first degree.

"Well, in my day we didn't just go to the store and buy pre-faded denim. We had to put our own holes in our jeans," he sour-graped wondering what the world was coming to. Victor switched stations with one hand as he pulled out into traffic without signaling — after all, he only had so many hands.

Doug stared out the window nervously.

On the drive to The Zone, Victor regaled Doug with tales of the original Twilight Zone after-hours club. He talked about it enthusiastically and wistfully. He'd still been married to Yolanda, but she'd been so engrossed in her work at Summerwood and Summerwood that she'd encouraged him to go out. Have fun. Leave her alone.

Like its namesake, this new Zone was located in an old warehouse, but unlike the old one, it featured more than a sound system, a bar and a unisex bathroom with the largest bottle of mouthwash ever made. To get to the new club, they rode up a huge, solid freight elevator, emerging on the third floor to the sound of the latest in alternative dance music.

Lots of people greeted Victor warmly; he felt quite touched by it. After all, he'd never been as much part of "the scene" as Maurice and Johnnie, and was pleasantly surprised that so many of their friends remembered him. He was equally pleased that many of Maurice's coworkers also welcomed him. After all, he was the boss's ex-husband; what did that count for now? It was kind of funny, actually, watching Yolanda's underlings try to decide if his ass was worth kissing. The gay half of the crowd seemed to have no such problem.

When Victor remembered a name, he introduced Doug; otherwise, he just sort of left his buddy to tag along. Most people, it seemed, wanted to meet Victor's good-looking companion — and not just the women, either.

Maurice's infamous brother Henri appeared out of the crowd and made sure they had drinks before wading further into the fête. Henri ignored Doug's protests about alcohol and insisted that he have some of the killer Kool-Aid. He said he was very impressed with Doug's discerning sense of taste and smell, because there really was very little alcohol in it — hardly any at all. He'd made it himself. Just a teeny, tiny bit of gin. And vodka. Reluctantly, nervously, Doug took a small sip, sputtered, then downed it like medicine. Henri promptly re-filled his glass, despite his protests otherwise.

"Victor! Doug! Over here!" Maurice's uncharacteristic screech cut through the party sounds of music and conversation. Doug seemed relieved to see people he knew and felt comfortable with. They headed for the birthday boy and his partner. The usually reasonable Maurice was obviously feeling no pain, as, in an odd bit of role-reversal, Johnnie was obviously the designated adult for the evening.

Maurice pulled Victor into a quick hug and peck on the lips. Doug glanced hurriedly at Johnnie, but the other man just grinned at his partner. Maurice grabbed Doug and gave him the same treatment, adding, "How's the best-looking guy in the place doing?" Doug blushed and took a big gulp of his drink, choking less this time.

A terribly efficient waiter just happened to cruise by at that moment, swapping Doug's half empty cup for a new and fuller glass from his tray.

"Uh-oh." Johnnie nudged Victor and gestured with his chin toward a couple over by the bar. It was Yolanda, leaning up into a tall, dark-haired, handsome man, nuzzling his neck and stroking his arm.

"She always was one for public displays of affection...when she was shit-faced," Victor sighed. "Guess that's the new boyfriend, right?"

"Sorry, Victor. He's a big corporate guy — VP of some big-bucks company, I'm afraid."

Scanning the crowd, Yolanda waved at Victor to come over, liquid sloshing over the sides of the glass in her gesturing hand.

"Guess I'd better go over and pay my disrespects." He took a deep breath.

"Do you want me to... I'll just wait here then, shall I? Yes. Right you are." Doug appeared to be talking to himself, because Victor certainly wasn't paying any attention as he placed his empty glass on a nearby table and headed over.

"Hiya, 'Landa." He hated the forlorn way his words sounded.

"Victor!" Yolanda, too, appeared to have been dipping into the hardly-any-alcohol-at-all spiked punch. "Victor!" She leaned up to try for a kiss on the lips, but he shifted his head slightly and she landed on his cheek instead. "Victor! This is Gordon Hewitt." She blinked owlishly and looked at him expectantly.

Just to be a shit, he held out his hand and said, "Hewitt. Hewitt. What team you play for?"

Hewitt's practiced-sincere handshake faltered. "Ah, no. I'm...I don't...That is, I..."

Yolanda giggled. "Good one, Victor. Gordon is almost a vice president at Standard Corporation." She rolled her eyes a little. "But he does look like a professional athlete, doesn't he?" She ran a possessive hand down her escort's arm.

Victor thought Hewitt could use a few less trips to the boardroom and a few more trips to the gym, but refrained from saying so. "Pleased to meet you. I'm the ex," he said instead.

The light-bulb look came on in Hewitt's eyes and he ran a quick look up and down Victor's much-more-fit body. A combination of surprise and disdain colored his yuppie features.

"We were very young," Yolanda explained; it sounded sadly like an apology. The leaden feeling that had occupied the lower part of Victor's belly suddenly flared hot and rough, like a molten bowling ball had taken up residence deep inside his gut. He wished he had another drink.

And just like that, Doug appeared at his side, warm hand on his arm, a drink offered to Victor, which he grabbed and quickly downed almost half of, awfully glad of the "teeny, tiny bit of gin. And vodka."

As the liquor burned down Victor's gullet, Doug extended his hand to Yolanda, then pulled it back quickly to wipe the condensation on his jeans, right next to his crotch. He extended it again, saying, "Hi. You must be Yolanda. You're every bit as lovely as Victor described." Yolanda took the hand, holding it much longer than necessary.

"And you would be?" she asked breathily.

"Oh. I'm sorry. I assumed you knew. I'm Doug. Doug Newkirk. Victor's...partner. Training partner," he amended with a crooked grin.

Victor watched in confusion, as Doug added, "We met at the gym." He placed his left hand against the small of Victor's back.

Hewitt coughed impatiently. "I don't believe I've had the pleasure." He reached out a hand to Doug. "Gordon Hewitt." A look of satisfaction settled on his face when Doug's face registered recognition. The two men shook.

"Ah, yes. I've done some work on your firm — Standard Corporation, isn't it? I'm an accountant — a *forensic* accountant, oftimes attached to the Canada Customs and Revenue Agency." He gazed levelly at Hewitt. "Specifically, the taxation branch." Hewitt looked uncomfortable.

Yolanda continued to gaze at Doug.

Conversation stuttered to a halt; awkward was the watchword of the moment. Johnnie appeared magically at the edge of their little circle doing the solicitous host thing — did anyone need drinks? Food? A cab home?

Doug had nudged right up against Victor, his arm now slung lazily around Victor's waist, stroking his hip lightly, possessively. Yolanda and Hewitt were both riveted on it.

Yolanda snapped her attention from Doug's drifting fingers to glare at Johnnie. "Oh, Gordon and I are fine, thank you." Her voice dripped sarcasm. "But I think Victor and his...friend need to get a room." If her eyes hadn't already been green...

Johnnie glanced knowingly at Doug and Victor, who were virtually joined at the hip and gazing into one another's eyes. Johnnie rolled his own, muttering "straight as a pretzel" almost too low for Victor to pick up with his peripheral hearing. "It's okay, Yolanda," he crooned. "You're just being a bitch 'cause Victor's boyfriend is better looking than yours."

Yolanda sputtered and Hewitt looked confused. Johnnie wisely swept Doug and Victor away from the happy couple before he could do any more damage to his partner's career, since Maurice worked for Yolanda's law firm and she had been known to be vindictive on occasion.

As they moved away from Victor's ex and her new beau, Doug hung onto Victor, making it twice as difficult for them to cut through the crowd of revelers.

"It's okay, Doug. You can let go now. I appreciate what you did back there, but I'm fine now."

Without letting go of Victor, Doug used his free hand to grab back the drink he'd brought for Victor and down the last bit. "But I thought you liked me?" Doug's smile was both provocative and insecure. He was obviously looking for reassurance and...making advances?

"I do like you. You don't have to ask. I just —"

"Good. Let's get another drink. Your glass appears to be empty." This time Doug more or less dragged Victor toward the punch table. He reluctantly let go of Victor long enough to grab a glass in each hand, but instead of handing one to Victor, he brought it to Victor's lips and tipped it slightly back. Startled, Victor had to quickly swallow or wear it — and he'd always been good at swallowing. He wrapped both hands around Doug's to steady the glass, as Doug's focus appeared to be lower.

"You spilled some, Victor." Doug leaned down to lick his friend's punch-dribbled chin.

"Doug. Doug. Doug! What's going on here? Who put you up to this?" Victor glanced around, feeling a little pissed-off as well as a little drunk, trying to see if he was the brunt of somebody's practical joke.

"Well, Maurice and Johnnie thought it would be a good idea." Victor snapped his gaze back to Doug's eyes; what little focus he had was definitely centered on Victor. "They said it wasn't fair that Yolanda was all over her new…friend, and that I should go over and pretend to be your…friend. I said I didn't want to deliberately mislead anyone, but they said just go do what I normally do when I'm with you, only a bit more so. So I did, and now I can't seem to stop." His tipsy babble was punctuated by owlish blinks. He reached for Victor, then confusedly focused on the drinks that occupied both hands. He appeared to have solved the problem by chugging the first one, then going for the other.

"Stop, Doug. Stop!" Victor grabbed the drink that headed toward Doug's open mouth and set both glasses back on the table. "I mean…just…you're not used to alcohol. And, and…" His feeble protests were silenced as Doug's mouth descended over his.

Doug kissed slowly, persuasively, tongue caressing and slicking Victor's surprised lips — lips that almost opened and accepted the insistent seduction. Then he grabbed both of Doug's wrists again and levered back from the other man. "No. Doug. No. Just…back off. Okay?"

Doug blinked at him, confusion evident. He almost looked like he was going to cry. Oh, God. A sappy drunk. Just what I need.

People were starting to stare…and comment:

"Well, shit, baby. I'll sure take you if he doesn't."

"I wouldn't be turning that down."

"There's always someone gets drunk and makes a scene."

Victor grabbed Doug's hand and dragged him toward the exit.

Knowing the area well, Victor hauled Doug down a narrow alley that would bring them swiftly to the lot where they'd left the car. Victor was still sober enough to drive, having had fewer than two drinks, cumulatively. Doug, however, decided he liked this alleyway just fine and flipped himself back against the wall, using surprise and momentum to pull Victor toward him — into his arms, against his body, between his widespread legs.

"Don't you want this?" He murmured into Victor's gel-crunchy hairline. "Don't you want me?"

Any protest died on Victor's lips when he felt Doug rub against him, a smooth slide that ran the length of his dick and brought it to hardness quick enough to make his head spin. And he had had nearly two drinks.

Caution be damned. "Oh, yeah! Doug. Baby." Ardent nonsense words escaped him, despite his resolve. After all, Doug had started this, hadn't he? He grabbed Doug's hips and mirrored the motion against Doug's hard cock. Doug hissed between clenched teeth and threw his head back, smacking it lightly on the brick wall behind him. "Yes," he hissed again, reassuring Victor before he could worry about the wall.

"Want you. Want you. Always wanted you." Victor's words spilled out, reassuring Doug and himself. He ground himself against his friend again.

Doug jabbed his hips into Victor's, all staccato out-of-control: not sophisticated and sensual, but dirty and sexy and inexperienced enough to be an incredible turn-on.

"Ohhhh," Doug moaned.

"Ohhhh," Doug moaned again, but this one didn't sound quite right to Victor. He pulled back, forcing himself to sober up as much as he could, stoned less on punch than on his own body chemistry: adrenaline, hormones, endorphins.

"Ohhhh, God. Going to be sick. Victor. Victor!" Doug started to lurch sideways down the wall. Victor grabbed him and bent him over so he'd miss their shoes — mostly.

Afterward, Doug sat shaking in the passenger seat, insisting he be dropped home rather than at Victor's apartment as suggested. He clearly asked Victor to leave after he'd helped the no-longer-quite-so-drunk man to bed. Jack lay flat on the mat beside the bed, whining a little in sympathy as Doug moaned softly and complained about whirling rooms.

"Got the spins, huh, Doug? Welcome to the exciting world of alcohol. Any wonder why it's so popular?" Victor moved the wastebasket close to the bed, putting two Aspirin, two Dramamine and two glasses of water on the nightstand.

"Not now. This is hardly the time for a lecture," Doug groaned.

"Sorry," Victor said, but he really didn't mean it. He felt more than a little under-appreciated at the moment. None of this was his fault, after all. It wasn't exactly flattering to have a guy kiss you, puke on you, and bitch you out all in the space of an hour. "I'm not sure I should leave you alone."

"That's just silly, Victor," Doug snapped, the effect ruined by the slightly slurred speech. "Now, please. Nobody ever died of a hangover. Well, unless there was alcohol poisoning involved, but we don't need to go into that right —"

Victor shoved the pills into Doug's mouth, followed by a short swallow of water to wash them down.

Doug choked a little, grabbed the water and drank the rest of it. "Thank you, but I'd really just like to be left alone now." In response to the whining coming from the side of the bed, Doug added, "No, you can stay, but I'll have no lectures from you either."

Jack quieted and returned nose to paws.

Victor hovered a bit longer, then, not entirely sure he was doing the right thing, finally let himself out of Doug's tiny apartment. He didn't feel so great himself, having been given the old one-two sucker punch to the gut tonight, first by Yolanda, then by Doug. God, he couldn't win for losing. He'd been thinking of getting another tattoo, what with them being so popular nowadays and all. Maybe something in a nice, Celtic *L*, centered on his forehead.

Shit. He'd have to call Maurice tomorrow and apologize. He headed home, where he almost gave in to the temptation to pull something hard and wet out of the liquor cabinet and get drunk himself. But years of experience with failed romance — Yolanda, Yolanda, and Yolanda — had taught him that alcohol only made things worse. He washed the cigarette-scented gel out of his hair and climbed into bed. Sleep was a long time coming — even after he had, twice, with sad thoughts of lovers lost to keep him company on that lonely journey.

Since both men worked and worked out at the gym, it seemed inevitable that they'd run into each other soon enough. Based on their two previous experiences with almost-sex, not-quite foreplay, Victor assumed Doug needed a couple of days to regroup and then they'd get takeout and talk and go back to training together. And besides, this time Doug had initiated the contact, so Victor was the injured party here. He worked up quite a head of righteous indignation. He went about his duties like an automaton. He missed his friend.

It was Nelly who inadvertently gave Victor the clue that Doug was actively avoiding him. "You guys have a fight? He checked your schedule and now he's coming in when you're not on. Does that mean he's up for grabs?" Hope against hope, Nelly. He always was. Victor thought he might be coming down with something. He felt his own forehead.

"You okay?" Nelly asked him from the mirror, where she was applying another layer of lip-gloss. "You don't look so good."

"You think? Maybe I should go home."

"I dunno, Victor. Maybe it's better for you to stay at work. I've been to your neighborhood."

※ ※ ※

When he couldn't stand it any longer, he called Doug. He got Doug's answering machine and left a stupid, rambling message he wished he could just erase. He flung his phonebook across the room, where it hit the wall and drifted down in sections. Well, the ball was in Doug's court now; he'd just have to sit and wait. He left two more barely coherent messages before giving up.

※ ※ ※

Victor started working longer and longer hours, despite Phil's insistence that he wouldn't get overtime pay for it. He came in early and dragged out his own workout, then stayed late doing every possible bit of paperwork. He engaged people in conversation, sometimes about steroids even when he knew they couldn't possibly be users or suppliers. He started tuning up the equipment, tidying up after rush hour, picking up the change room. He even found himself polishing the water fountain; the place had never been so orderly. But, despite his best efforts, he failed to make the hoped-for rendezvous.

One Sunday morning, Phil mentioned that Doug hadn't shown to go over the books, nor had he called. This was so unlike Doug that even Phil noticed. Victor volunteered to stop by Doug's apartment to check up on him.

Doug answered the door wearing jeans and a shirt unbuttoned as if hastily donned. His hair was tousled, his lips slightly swollen, and his feet bare. He opened the door partway.

"Hey, Doug. You okay?" Victor was concerned. Doug didn't look himself.

"Morning, Victor." Doug smiled muzzily, rubbing slight stubble with the hand not bracing the door half-shut. Doug seemed glad to see him. Or at least he wasn't pissed.

"Phil said you didn't show, didn't call, so I figured you had to be pretty sick. You all right?"

"I'm fine."

A glance at the sound of a door opening down the hall told Victor that Mr. Nbizzlemeiner the dog-sitter was home and prying. "So you're not sick, then?"

"No, I'm fine. Thanks for asking." Doug started to close the door. Victor put his hand on the frame.

"But you didn't go to work?"

"Must have slept in." What was with Doug? He never slept in.

"Are you in some kind of trouble?"

"No. No, no, no, no…I just…I have a friend visiting."

"Oh. What kind of friend? A guy friend? Girl friend?" Victor hated himself immediately for asking.

Doug shuffled his feet uncomfortably. "Well, I, er…"

"You're not alone? You missed work to fuck?" Victor's voice squeaked with incredulity.

Doug eyed Victor's hand on the doorframe pointedly. Victor refused to move it, knowing Doug would never hurt him and so couldn't close the door. "Yes."

"Unbelievable." Victor ran a hand through his hair, forgetting that he'd worn it straight this morning. Not straight anymore, though. Although some things obviously were.

Doug started to look a little insulted. "Why unbelievable, Victor. That I would be able to attract the attentions and affection of a woman? A beautiful woman, as a matter of fact. I did mention I was straight at some point, didn't I?" Sarcasm City, and Doug's the mayor.

"Yeah, you did, Doug. I just wasn't listening, I guess."

Doug took another stab at closing the door. Taking the hint this time, Victor dropped his hand and stepped back. "Thanks for dropping by, Victor."

Turning to leave, Victor watched Mr. Nbizzlemeiner eavesdropping unrepentantly from his doorway. "He's found someone," Victor informed him in a whisper. He leaned back against the now-closed door, shamelessly listening himself. A woman's voice, soft and sultry said, "Do you really have to go to work?"

"Yeah." Doug's voice was husky. Victor thought he heard a twinge of guilt in it. Or was that just wishful thinking? "Kind of…although…since I am self-employed, I think I can decide if I need to take a sick day…or two."

The last thing Victor heard before he stumbled past Mr. Nbizzlemeiner was the woman's voice, saying, "You do look a little flushed. I think you should go straight back to bed."

I COULD HAVE BEEN A PRETENDER

It was nearly a month later when Victor heard Doug's voice coming from the gym owner's office. He started to sweat a little as he tried to decide what to do. His shift was long over, but he was still hanging around.

When Doug finally emerged from Veronica's office, he was laughing. She must have walked him to the door, because he turned back to her — and leaned in for a kiss! Her eyes never left his face as their lips touched briefly. Doug closed his eyes and looked totally smitten. Now Victor knew for certain he was coming down with something, because he suddenly felt sick to his stomach.

Victor wanted to flee, but Veronica turned back into her office and Doug looked up, right at Victor. Victor did the next best thing, which was to go for cool. He turned his attention back to his paperwork and focused on trying to breathe.

Peripherally, he watched Doug hesitate a moment and then head toward him with determined gait. "Hello, Victor." Doug's tone was serious; there was no joy at seeing him.

"Hey, Doug." Victor just felt sad and defeated.

"I've been meaning to talk to you. I know I owe you a phone call." Or several, thought Victor uncharitably.

"You don't owe me nothin', Doug. You were straight with me right from the beginning. Literally." Victor's tone was humorless. "I just thought you were kidding yourself there for a while, but I can see you've got everything straightened out." Veronica re-emerged from her office and stood leaning on the doorframe watching them, a wintry smile playing around her pretty mouth.

"I'm sorry, Victor. I thought we could be friends, but I've talked about it with Veronica and she thinks it's cruel for me to keep you...hanging on." Victor had an urge to go home and listen to old Motown till he felt better — like maybe next year.

"So you and Veronica, then?"

Doug nodded.

"How long?" He had to know. He had to know.

"Just a few weeks. After I...you...Maurice's party. I never would have cheated on my significant other if we'd been involved at the time."

Victor felt hope well up in his chest at the way this sentence was worded, but squashed it quickly down. He knew what Doug was trying to say: that he never would have kissed Victor if he'd already been involved with Veronica, and not the other way around.

"So it's serious, then?" Stop asking stupid, personal questions, Victor admonished himself. But he knew he'd continue to ask as long as Doug would answer.

"We're taking it slow. We don't want to rush into anything."

"Well, buddy." Victor tried out an impersonal nickname, the kind of thing he used when he couldn't remember someone's name. "Don't let me keep you." He tried to look busy, but he was so up-to-date on his paperwork there really wasn't anything he could do. Doug continued to stand there, shifting uneasily from foot to foot. Veronica had disappeared back into her office, apparently satisfied with the damage being done.

Doug *ahem*'ed softly, and Victor finally put down his pen and looked at him again. "Is there something I can do for you, Doug?" Damn. Slipped back into the first name again. Damn. Damn.

"Well, actually there is." Doug looked uncomfortable but determined to see through his mission.

Victor raised an eyebrow and crossed his arms over his chest. No point in making this easy for the guy who had dumped him. Although they'd never actually been together, so... "What?"

"Well, Veronica told me that you and she had a conversation a while back about steroid use here at Orr's Gym. She knows you've been asking around on her behalf as she requested, but she wanted you to know that it's okay now. You can stop asking. She's got it under control."

"What? Was I driving away her customers?" Victor was suddenly furious. What the fuck kind of bullshit had this woman been feeding Doug?

Doug blinked rapidly. "No. I don't think the sale of gym memberships has been affected. It's just that she's worried it might make some clients uncomfortable. I remember how you mentioned it to me on my very first visit." He paused, scratching the old scar in his eyebrow. Something about that small gesture just about broke Victor's heart. Doug continued, "And while she certainly appreciates the thought, she'd like you to please stop talking about steroids now."

"And she couldn't tell me herself? After all, she is my boss, right?"

"Well, no, Victor. Actually, Phil's your boss. Veronica is your manager-once-removed."

"Great. Now you know more about my job than I do."

"Well, I do work here as well, Victor. In a slightly more managerial capacity than you." This was getting nasty, unnecessarily so. Victor reined in his temper.

"Right, then. No more talk of 'roids. Tell the boss lady she's got it."

"Victor?" Tentative.

"What?" Sulky. Sarcastic.

"You're not" — deep breath, huge breath — "the one selling…"

"What?"

"No. Of course not. It's just that Veronica said… You're not, are you, Victor? You do seem to know a lot about them."

Victor stared angrily, furiously at Doug for a long moment, chest heaving with pain and wounded pride and the need to control his temper. He felt his eyes start to prickle, and shook his head fiercely. How could Doug? After everything?

Doug smiled grimly, his eyes almost meeting Victor's as he thanked him and turned to leave. Victor had to speak, had to say what he felt, that he cared. Gathering his fraying dignity around him like a gym towel, he said to the retreating back, "Oh, and Doug?"

Doug turned halfway back. "Yes?"

"Be careful. Some predators survive by blending in."

Doug looked puzzled, but thanked Victor again and this time left the floor.

Once Doug was clearly out of both sight and earshot, Veronica sauntered over to the counter where Victor stared grimly after his former friend. She startled him by dropping her cold hand over his.

"Nervous, Victor?" He felt she could see directly into his brain...his heart...his soul. His palm began to sweat where she pressed it against the laminate countertop.

She laughed, not a pleasant sound. "So how's the love life?" She leaned an elbow on the counter across from him, resting chin on palm. She blinked up at him as if she cared.

"Veronica," he pleaded. "He's new at all this. Please don't —"

"Don't what, Victor? Hurt him? Play with him? Lead him on?" If words could bite, he'd be missing large chunks. "I told you I had a long memory!" She dug her icy fingers into his hand, holding his eyes, then dropped his hand abruptly. She swaggered back to her office, knowing she'd won this particular battle of the sexes.

✕ ✕ ✕

Victor continued to come to work every day, talking to people about their health and fitness, programs and progress, who was dealing in what. He was buddies with everyone: *friends, juice-heads, countrymen, tell me your problems. I'm all ears.*

He'd tried talking about his own issues: "You ever feel like you don't know who you are? That your entire life you've been defined by your wife, your friends, your job? You ever feel like that?"

He received no helpful responses, and a few rather unhelpful ones:

"No. I never feel that way. That's just weird."

"No. We're not getting back together, Victor."

"Yes. All the time. Life's not worth living, is it?" He gently provided the suicide hotline number to the latter.

He seemed to be making headway on the friend front; people were coming to trust him, confide in him. Phil appointed him acting assistant manager and even let him talk to potential new customers on Phil's days off, although most of the commission went into the Phil Martini fund for more Day-Glo tracksuits. Still, Victor didn't mind. It gave him all the more reason to hang around the gym, and money had never been the object of his job at Orr's.

✕ ✕ ✕

One night a few weeks after he and Doug had had their little no-more-steroid-talk talk, Victor was sitting in Phil's office going over the schedule for the following week. It was late and he'd thought he was the only staff member on the main floor when he heard raised voices through the thin walls.

He knew Doug's new cubbyhole of an office was on the other side of the wall, entered from the aerobics area, but he hadn't realized Doug was also working late. When had he stopped being focused on his former friend? Oh, yeah. About the time he rededicated himself to the job he was supposed to be doing here.

Since Doug was being compensated with a complimentary gym membership, Veronica had seen fit to maximize all the no-charge accounting services she could get. Free accounting services were a profitable trade-off when weighed against the minor revenue generated by the tanning room Doug's office had been just a few weeks ago. Besides, there were still three others. The renovations had been hasty; the bare wires from the tanning bed still dangled menacingly behind Doug's tiny desk. Victor had commented to Phil about it not being up to code; Phil had said he'd get right on it — two weeks ago.

Now Victor froze, listening carefully as the voices escalated. Victor moved soundlessly to the heating vent near the floor of Phil's office — he could hear a lot clearer there.

"…must report this to the proper authorities, Veronica. I'm sure they'll understand. Someone has been using you, abusing your trust. Using this place to sell illegal anabolic steroids."

Victor grabbed a couple of things from his gym bag and crept silently around the corner from the reception area to the deserted aerobics room. He didn't need to get close to Doug's tiny office to see inside; the gigantic mirror blanketing the entire wall opposite him reflected the interior of Doug's office clearly. That gym rat habit of watching things indirectly in mirrors was paying off big time.

"Of course they're not mine, Doug. I have no idea how they got into that cupboard, but we can't involve the police. They'll confiscate them and, um, the real drug dealers would get mad and probably hurt us or kill us." Her voice climbed in register. "Or worse. They might mistakenly believe they're mine!""I've had professional dealings with both the Ontario Provincial Police and the Mounties. I'm sure they'll understand if we just explain it to them. In the meantime, I'll take these with me now to the local precinct. I believe it's just a few blocks from here."

Victor watched as Doug started to lift a large box and head to the door. Veronica moved on stockinged feet to block his path.

Cool now, but with regret obvious in her tone. "I can't let you do that, Doug. Please put down the box."

"But, Veronica. This is the best way. Don't you see?"

"I see you taking a huge amount of money from my pocket, is what I see."

Doug gasped. Placing the box on the desk again, he took a step toward Veronica.

"Veronica, please! What are you trying to say?"

"Oh, come off it, Doug. Nobody's that naïve. I'm the steroid dealer around here. Don't you get that?"

"You're saying you're a criminal?"

"What?" She gestured around her. "You think I can afford this lifestyle on the pittance I make with this gym? Pul-eeze. There's no money in running a gym. Why do you think they go belly-up all the time?"

Doug looked grim, but determined. "I'm sorry, Veronica. I don't want to do this, but that's tantamount to a confession. I'm going to have to make a citizen's arrest and take you into custody."

"I'm sorry, too, Doug. You were a great accountant, and great in bed, too." She drew a tiny revolver from her suit jacket pocket and pointed it at him. "Now pick up that box; we're going for a little ride. We'll just stop at my office for my shoes."

Both heads snapped up as Victor appeared framed in the office doorway, shouting, "Freeze! Toronto Police!" Victor's own gun, held in both hands, was aimed directly at Veronica's heart.

In a flash, Veronica jumped behind Doug and pointed her gun at his neck. "Still trying to get attention, eh, Victor?" She jabbed the gun hard just below Doug's ear. "If you don't back off right now, pretty boy here isn't going to look so good anymore."

"Okay. Okay, Veronica. Whatever you want." Victor lowered the gun a little, panting as he tried to think. What to do? What to do? Victor watched Doug closely, plans and ideas quickly being reviewed and discarded. At last he said to Doug, "It's okay to be scared, Doug. I'm scared myself. In fact, I haven't been this scared since I was caught up in that grocery store robbery I told you about." A single bead of sweat trickled from his brow, oiling the way as he ran a conspiratorial thumb down his nose. "You remember my robbery story, don't you, Doug?"

Veronica slid her gun up under Doug's jaw, the first few millimeters of the barrel sinking into the soft flesh.

Please. Please. Please remember the story! Victor had done his best; rest was up to Doug. He frantically sought a contingency plan in case Doug didn't get it.

As he watched, Victor saw the fear in Doug's eyes slowly replaced by the dawn of understanding and hope. Victor prayed he wasn't imagining it — 'cause there'd be no nod of acknowledgement, no sly answering thumb running down the side of that attractive nose.

Then he heard it: heard the soft susurration of trickling liquid, and he knew — Doug had got it.

Oh, yuck. Veronica eased her hold on Doug and hopped quickly back from the disgusting yellow puddle that was pooling around her stocking feet. Doug's eyes never left Victor's; a look of pride suffused his features.

Holding his gun before him like a beacon, Victor advanced on Veronica, who withdrew further into the tiny room. Her wet bare feet hit the cable that connected Doug's laptop to the outlet in the wall behind her. She flailed wildly to keep her balance, her gun hand squeezing the trigger and the other reaching blindly behind her searching for support. Toward the wall. Toward the bare dangling wires.

Then everything was confusion: a blinding flash of light — sparks like fireworks on Canada Day. Somebody screamed; hell, everybody screamed! Popping sounds, sizzling sounds. Clouds of smoke. Horrible smell of burning, charring. A glimpse of Doug, wearing running shoes on his hands like amputee gloves, reaching the far wall, patting at flames, gently lowering something to the floor.

Victor faded in and out of awareness, the pain of the bullet that had ripped through his thigh unbearable. It wasn't the first time he'd been shot in the line of duty, but fuck, man, it's not like you build up a tolerance or anything. Doug bent over him, cradling him tenderly, whispering encouragement. "It's a good thing," Victor managed, "that you keep your dad's old hip flask full of Gatorade in your pocket."

Doug's "Don't try and talk, Victor," seemed like excellent advice. He took a deep breath; the stink of ozone and smoke filled his lungs. He turned his head to one side to cough weakly.

Across the way he saw paramedics (and when had they gotten there?) ministering to the blackened thing on the gurney in the corner. Oh, God! His stomach soured at the horrific sight of Veronica, that magnificent mane now a crispy halo framing her dazed and sooty face. He slid into darkness to the smell of burning hair.

Victor dropped onto the old wooden bench, crutches rattling, wondering briefly just how many criminal butts had polished it. He kept telling his physiotherapist he was okay without the crutches now, but she just stared at him, Yoda-like, over her funky designer-frame glasses. The Crown attorney thought the crutches were a great way to get court sympathy for her case, which made Victor feel guilty for using them, but after a long day on harsh seats he was more than glad he'd brought them. Using them with a suit jacket on was a bitch, though; his old tweedy sports jacket rucked up under his arms, and the extra bulk caused chafing like his hockey gear never had.

"Victor."

Victor craned his neck to look up at the man hovering over him, then turned away again, blowing out his cheeks in a long-suffering breath. He'd managed to avoid speaking with Doug at all for the duration of the trial, but there was no getting out of it this time. "What is it, Doug?"

"I just thought…well, that is, I wondered…no, I'll just ask. Can I be of any assistance, Victor?"

"No. I'm fine." He stared straight ahead. "Thanks anyway."

The silence grew; the musty scent of the old marble corridor tickled Victor's allergies. A clock that reminded him uncomfortably of chalk-dusty classrooms ticked loudly above them.

Doug moved into Victor's line of vision. Victor looked over at the closed courtroom doors.

"Mind if I sit down?"

"It's a free country."

Doug shifted on his feet like a prize-fighter, or a five-year-old in need of a bathroom, finally seating himself a couple of feet away on the wooden bench. It creaked loudly in the silence, competing with the clock.

Tick. Tock. Creak. Victor snuffled, wiping his nose on his sleeve. A radiator sighed loudly, blowing off a little steam. Or maybe that was Victor.

Like synchronized swimmers, both bench occupants swung their heads to the right at the sound of footsteps. They watched a uniformed cop escort a mild-looking man up the long corridor, past them and away again, handcuffs glinting under each grill-covered window set high near the ceiling. The footsteps echoed loudly in the empty corridor.

Victor stared, unseeing, long after the moving tableau had passed. He started when Doug finally broke the painful silence. "I guess you'll be glad to get all this behind you. Return to your real job at the Metro Toronto Police Department."

Victor hunched over, elbows resting on knees even though it caused the healing bullet wound in his thigh some discomfort. He gazed at his clasped hands, his own knees, anywhere but at the man seated beside him.

"Victor?"

Victor leaned back tiredly, smacking his head lightly on the seat's high wooden back. It reminded him far too much of the bench outside the principal's office at his high school. He sighed again, rolling his head toward Doug. "What do you want, Doug?"

"I...nothing. I just wanted to... I miss you, Victor. I miss my friend."

Victor finally took a good look at his former friend. Doug looked awful. He was wearing that much-too-large and much-too-outdated pinstripe suit Victor had once made him change out of. The night of the alleyway. The night of Maurice's birthday party, he corrected himself.

Never mind, Victor told himself, and rolled his head back to its original position, eyes front. "We were never friends, Doug. I was undercover. You were a potential witness. That's all it was.

That's all it ever was. When we get a verdict, pretty soon, I hope, I'll go my way and you'll go yours and that, my not-friend, will be that." He screwed his eyes shut and scrubbed his hands over his face. His previously mild headache abruptly loomed large behind his closed eyes.

He heard Doug stand to leave, then Victor's eyes flew open again at the loud clash of courtroom doors thrown wide. The court clerk called Doug back in, leaving Victor alone in the hallway again.

※ ※ ※

The judge spent several more hours in examination, discussion, and deliberation. Victor, as the arresting officer, was called back to the stand twice for clarification of testimony. Doug, the star witness, was dismissed after one final examination. He returned for the verdict, however, although Victor absolutely refused to look over his shoulder to check — more than once. Finally, Veronica was directed to stand and receive her judgment.

"Guilty!" the judge pronounced, and Veronica Amorotique received a fairly stiff sentence for a first offence in illegal trafficking of controlled substances, along with a second, longer sentence, to be served concurrently, for shooting a police officer. With a resounding bang, the gavel hit the little oaken disk, and the courtroom was cleared.

Veronica glared at the judge, at the court clerk, and at the guard who moved to escort her back to the holding cells. She completely ignored Victor and Doug. As she turned to leave, she tossed her head to one side as if she still had her old cascade of curls, but only succeeded in unseating her flimsy cotton headscarf. A little of the frizzy, baby-fine new growth showed at the front as she tried to pull it back into place, rendered clumsy by the handcuffs. She was still struggling with the scarf as the guard led her away.

Victor stood, stretched and surveyed the courtroom as the rest of the audience and officials packed up and filed out. Several reporters, ignoring the black looks of the court clerk, were already on cell phones.

Glad to be heading out and putting all this behind him, Victor reached inside himself for that feeling of triumph he was entitled to after nailing a perp, but found only hollowness. He hobbled out, keeping his eyes on his footing.

Daylight faded rapidly in these last days of November. Victor stood at the corner near the courthouse trying to flag a cab in rush-hour traffic. "Give a gimp a break," he thought as he stepped off the curb in the vain hope of catching the next taxi, but instead of stopping, it swerved to go around the man waving the crutch, honking as it passed. He ignored the honking and groaned at the pain where the remaining crutch chafed him under his arm, echoing that of his leg and his head. He knew he looked like Tiny Tim — from Dickens, not *Laugh-In*. "God bless this, asshole!" he yelled as yet another taxi refused to stop. He'd have grabbed his crotch for effect if he'd had a free hand.

Another honk and he'd had enough. He rounded on the driver, prepared to see if a crutch could take on a windshield, when he recognized the handsome face thrust dangerously out into Bay Street traffic.

"Get in, Victor."

Victor didn't need to be told twice.

He hopped to the passenger side like a one-legged bunny, just as Doug opened it for him. He flung himself into the seat and sighed noisily with relief. His armpit felt better the instant the pressure was off, and his head felt better too, despite the continued honking. Escalating honking, actually. He looked around. "Why aren't we moving, Doug?"

"Seat belt, Victor. I would think that as a police officer…"

Click. "Okay, go."

Doug signaled and pulled away from the curb. A bit more honking and they were underway. "Still live on Queen?"

It hasn't been that long, Doug. Jeez. Out loud he said, "Yeah. I still do." He stared out the passenger side window as they drove in silence up Bay, headed east on Dundas, then back down again.

"Take Adelaide. Better in this traffic," was the sum total of Victor's input, despite several attempts on Doug's part to make conversation. Eventually Doug turned on the radio, where some alternative rocker whined on about something angsty. Probably love. Victor tapped his foot once before being painfully reminded of his not-quite-healed gunshot wound.

Traffic sucked. It took almost twenty-five uncomfortable minutes to reach the parking lot outside Victor's building. Although it was barely five thirty, full winter dark had set in. Doug pulled into the unexpectedly vacant guest spot and killed the engine.

"Thanks for the lift. I appreciate it." Victor put one hand on the door handle, but made no further move to exit. He dreaded the three flights of stairs, and allowed curiosity and a desire to stall for a few more minutes to overcome his resolve. "When'd you get a car, anyway?"

"I borrowed it. It belongs to Phil Martini at Orr's."

Trust Phil to have the radio set to some shit music station. "You still working there? After everything?"

"Not working there, no. But I still work out there, and Phil said he needed the money, so he loaned it to me for a small fee. Orr's is under new management now, you know."

Victor chuckled. "'For a small fee.' Probably more than this old shitbox is worth. What is it, '74? '75?" Almost old enough to be a classic, if anyone collected Gremlins. He surveyed the shabby interior, the old bench seat shifting slightly.

"Victor." Whoa. Suddenly Doug was a lot closer than a second ago. It had been Doug's weight that had rocked the front seat as he'd slid up close and personal. "Victor." Again. Breathily. "Are you in a hurry, Victor?" Doug murmured almost into Victor's ear.

Too shocked to react, Victor just stared at this new guy who looked exactly like Doug. Straight Doug. Self-proclaimed straight Doug. Doug took advantage of Victor's paralysis to close the distance between them, bringing his lips down over Victor's with delightful accuracy: no slipping off onto cheeks or painful clinking of teeth, despite the awkward position. Victor's mouth opened for less than a second, then he pulled away quickly, smacking the back of his head resoundingly on the window glass, his mouth still open, but definitely in astonishment rather than welcome.

"But you don't...you've never... Well...you don't kiss men," he finally choked out, shocked and surprised by this bizzaro mirror world he'd found himself in.

Doug smiled tentatively. "I miss you, Victor. I..."

Taking pity on the struggling man, Victor threw him a lifeline. "You'd do anything to get me back? To have things back the way they were?"

Despite the early-evening shadows, Victor could clearly see the look of relief wash over Doug's face. "Thank you for understanding, Victor. I..." Then Doug shocked Victor anew by running his left hand rapidly up Victor's thigh and setting it down firmly on his crotch.

With grim determination Victor moved his left hand from between them, grabbing Doug's deftly massaging one and shifted it back to Doug's own thigh, holding it there.

Victor looked questioning, "Doug? I'm kind of at a loss here... You said you were straight. Liked women. What are you doing?"

"I'm...I'm..." Third time's the charm. "I'm getting in touch with my homosexual side, Victor." Doug drew a deep breath and met Victor's eyes. He glanced meaningfully to where Victor's hand still pinned his firmly on his thigh. Victor followed his gaze and moved his hand quickly as if burned, then brought it down on Doug's crotch, taking a moment to feel the unmistakable woody beneath the baggy gabardine slacks.

"Well, maybe you are at that." He gave one final squeeze before withdrawing his hand, eliciting the tiniest of thrusts and gasps. "But it's too little, too late." Well, hardly too little from what he'd felt, but definitely too late.

He exited the car with as much dignity as a man can with crutches and a hard-on. His headache was back, pounding so loudly he could hardly hear Doug's litany of apologies. Inside, the stairs loomed ahead of him like Everest. He shook his throbbing head to clear it, immediately sorry he had. Taking a deep breath, he started up the stairs, stairs that seemed a little blurry at times.

PENANCE, ANYONE?

Three weeks after the trial, Victor found himself channel surfing until his thumb was sore. Sorer than his leg, he noted as he swung himself off the sofa and headed for the kitchen with barely a limp. He grabbed another beer, the third or fourth of the evening. He'd missed beer while he'd been on prescription painkillers; he much preferred the general anesthetic dispensed by The Beer Store. He was even looking forward to getting back to work on Monday, although he was restricted to desk duty for another couple of weeks. "Good as new," he'd told the doctor when he'd been examined earlier that day. "Almost," she'd replied, signing him back to work anyway, but not before eliciting his promise to keep up the physio for six more weeks, and then they'd see about him returning to his regular workouts. He missed those, too. Missed Orr's. Missed...

His head felt a little fuzzy and he considered switching to fruit juice — after this beer, of course. Hey, it was already open. He glanced at the phone as he headed back to the couch, feeling like a little human contact, but not sure whom he could call. He'd never quite rebuilt his social life after he and Yolanda split. She'd gotten most of their friends in the divorce, along with the better couch and good silver. Not that he cared. No, really.

After the trial separation (*trial*, hah!), he'd toyed with the idea of leaving town, maybe moving to Florida. He had family there. Hell, who in Canada didn't? He sure wouldn't miss winter. But that would have entailed another round of paperwork, the hassle of relocation, re-certifying to qualify for police work in another country. It was the thought of being busted back to uniform again that stopped him from even contemplating heading south. Plus, he liked Canada: improved government support systems, socialized medical care, same-sex marriage and common-law benefits mandated by the government. Hell, even abortion virtually on demand — no back-alley butcher jobs like

Yolanda had had back in the day. Hard to walk away from. Not to mention the fact that he really liked poutine.

So instead of making new friends or moving away after the divorce, he'd thrown himself into his job, and undercover assignments certainly didn't make for lasting relationships. His ability to do make-believe left him with nothing but imaginary friends. Well, there was always Maurice and Johnnie. He glanced at the clock on his VCR, which still flashed *12:00, 12:00, 12:00.* He didn't actually know what time it was, since he'd had nothing on his slate today except the doctor's appointment at ten this morning. He knew it was Friday after sundown, but nothing more precise than that.

He thought briefly about jacking off. Sex on a Friday night; Johnnie would say it's a mitzvah. Or were you supposed to have a partner for it to count?

He didn't feel very interested, but figured a porno flick could change that quick enough. He sifted through his gay porn: "When Hairy Met Studly," "Three Men and Oh, Baby!" "Masterbators of the Universe," "Terms of Endowment," "The Iceman Cummeth." He briefly considered the seasonal hit "Ebenezer Screwed," but figured he'd wait until Christmas for that one. He even glanced at straight porn: "Tales of the Clitty," and "Titty Titty Gang Bang." After all, a change was as good as a rest, right?

It wasn't a great collection, and nothing really sparked his interest. As he was putting them back in alphabetical order, by kink, he spied a lone video off to one side. It was "A Mountie Always Does His Man," the film he'd come home to find Doug watching all those months ago.

Doug. The very thought had him wavering on his feet for a moment, feeling like he'd just taken a shot to the gut. Really, really hard. He told himself to get a grip. Told himself it was just a job. Told himself to move on. He inserted the video in the VCR and sprawled back on the couch to watch. He was going to jerk off to this movie if it was the last thing he ever did.

He grabbed his dick though his track pants and began to manipulate it while the jumpy opening credits displayed a virtual catalogue of typefaces. By the time the first hard dick appeared on screen, his still wasn't, and he knew this was going to be a challenge, like shooting pool with a rope.

Eventually he got a good groove going. He was, after all, a guy, so a broken heart didn't necessarily mean a broken dick. Victor was having trouble focusing and blamed the beer — increases the desire while it screws up the performance.

He was just moving from self-teasing to some serious whacking when a rap on the apartment door startled him into knocking his empty beer bottle across the floor, and set his heart racing like it should have been a second earlier.

Moving on instinct, he crossed the small apartment twice; first to fetch his gun from the closet, and again to stand to one side of the door as he called out, "Who's there?"

"It's me, Victor."

Oh fuck. Doug. What's he doing here?

A quick glance downward reassured him his hard-on had dissipated, but not without leaving a tiny dark spot where he'd leaked a little. Or maybe it was beer. What the hell, if he couldn't tell what it was, Doug certainly couldn't either. He wasn't about to get all bent out of shape just because…

"May I come in, Victor?"

Right. Right. Door. Got it. He released the lock, swung open the door, and Doug stepped into the hallway. Unlike last time Victor had seen him, when he'd been dressed in that crappy old suit for court, this time Doug wore his Victor-clone best: black ripped jeans despite the November temperatures and a navy shirt of some kind. Victor couldn't tell with the black leather jacket that he didn't offer to take. "You coming in?" he asked, feeling somehow that the decision was Doug's, the fact that it was Victor's apartment notwithstanding.

Without waiting for an answer Victor crossed the apartment twice more, replacing the gun, snatching two cold beers from the fridge and setting them open on the coffee table. He sprawled on the couch again, one foot up beside the beer that wasn't in his hand, and the other flat on the floor. He glued his eyes back on the porn flick that had continued to run; Doug could take up the implied offer or go. Victor resolutely didn't care, no matter how he felt.

What he did feel was a little vindicated and a little nauseated when the couch cushions on his left gave under Doug's weight. His lousy peripheral vision showed him only a white blur heading toward the beer and a bottle-shaped blur heading back. They watched the final half hour of the film in relative silence punctuated only by heavy breathing and a fair amount of shifting and fidgeting from both parties.

⌘ ⌘ ⌘

The movie ended, the credits rolled. And they must have been the most fascinating credits ever, to judge by the intensity of the two men staring steadily at the TV. Once the snow started, with its irritating static, Victor switched off the VCR. An old black and white movie was playing on regular TV: once again the annoying ghost haunted poor, beleaguered Mrs. Muir, butting in at the worst possible moments, offering crappy, unwanted advice and ruining any hope she had of getting on with her life. Victor seized the TV guide and studied it like he was the next contestant on *Jeopardy*. Eventually, Doug rose and left the room.

Victor listened indifferently as his guest used the bathroom and then headed...into his bedroom. What the...? Victor waited a few minutes, and when Doug didn't return he put down the crossword he hadn't even started — what's a four-letter word for optimism? — and followed.

"Doug?" He felt weird knocking on his own bedroom door, but maybe the guy was sick or something and went to lie down. Doug had gotten really drunk on spiked punch that time, but one beer? Well, maybe he'd had a lot to drink before showing up at Victor's apartment. Dutch courage and all that. "You okay?" His eyes adjusted to the light, and he sucked in a breath so hard he nearly swallowed his tongue. *Don't*, he told himself, *you might need it later.*

Doug was indeed lying down, on his bed, buck naked. Wow. Buck naked. Lying face down on his bed. Buck naked. A survey of the moonlit room showed him Doug's clothes piled neatly on the bureau, bedspread folded at the foot of the bed, and Doug. Lying. On the bed. His bed. Buck fucking, butt-fucking naked!

Victor felt instantly aroused. Victor felt light-headed. Victor felt…scared as hell. A four-letter word for optimism? The answer's *hope*, which, much like Victor's dick, springs eternal.

"You okay?" Victor repeated, needing a couple of tries before anything recognizable as words emerged.

"I'm fine, Victor. Why don't you come over here and see for yourself?" The tremble in Doug's voice ruined the seductive effect Victor figured Doug was going for. He went over anyway. Hell, he couldn't have stayed away if he'd wanted to. And he almost thought he wanted to.

Victor stood nervously beside his bed, shifting from foot to foot, boxing, dancing, deciding.

"Take your clothes off, Victor."

Victor was naked almost before Doug could move, but not quite. Doug had time to get himself up on his knees and elbows, face hidden in the bedding. Victor froze when he saw this praying statue offered up on his sheets.

"What the fuck is this, Doug?" he ground out from between clenched teeth.

"Go ahead, Victor. It's all right. You deserve it. I deserve it," the supplicant mumbled into Victor's mousse-stained pillow.

"Ohhhh-kay." Victor climbed uncertainly onto the bed near Doug's proffered backside. "I'm just supposed to fuck you like this? No foreplay? No preparation? No condom, for Chrissake?"

It took Victor a minute to decipher "I thought you wanted it," from Doug's pillow talk.

"I did. I do. I… What? I'm just supposed to come up behind you and shove it in?" He raised one hand, palm up, but his gesture of confusion was lost on the man with the pillow on his head. He dropped the hand onto Doug's ass.

And Doug just about jumped out of his skin, and continued to tremble long after he'd re-positioned himself on his knees.

"Oh. My. God. Is this what hockey-boy did to you?" Doug responded with a shudder that may have involved a nod. "No wonder you hated it. No wonder there was blood. Did he even use any lubricant?" Doug jerked his shrouded head in the general direction of the nightstand, where a small bottle stood like a lone sentry.

Victor stretched over to grab it, leaning on Doug's hip for support, bringing the container close enough to read in the dim light. Doug shivered anew. Victor settled back, leaving his arm braced on Doug's hip. The hip felt unnaturally cool to the touch. "Baby oil," Victor mused. "Well, better than nothing. Although hardly as good as commercial products like Wet or even KY Jelly. And it'll wreck a condom."

Doug's face surfaced, natural curiosity apparently overcoming conditioned fear.

"What?" Victor continued chattily, dragging himself over to the other side of the bed, newly healed leg barely twinging, and settling in as if conversing naked with Doug was an everyday thing. Perhaps if he played this right it could be. "You think the drug companies would miss out on a potential market like that? Nah. After they figured out the nurses were raiding the medical supplies to use their slippery stuff as sexual lubricant, they re-packaged it, jacked up the price, and sold it to the general public. I remember finding my mom's *Personal Lubricant for the Married Lady* when I was just a kid." Victor's turn to shudder, but he soldiered on. "'Course now it's sold all over. In flavors. Yup. Flavors. Cherry's my favorite."

Doug looked thoughtful, despite Victor's lewd eyebrow waggle. Victor stoked a hand down Doug's broad lats, eliciting another flinch. Doug dove into the pillow once more. Maybe Victor should get him a security blanket.

"Relax, Doug." Doug didn't. "I am not going to fuck you." The handsome face emerged again, slowly, like a groundhog fearful of his shadow. "Well, I am." Oops. Six more weeks of winter. "But not like this. A guy wants a little foreplay, you know. C'mere." He pressed firmly on the small of Doug's back until the trembling man let himself be pushed flat on the bed, then Victor bodily wrestled Doug over on his side, facing him. Finally, Doug got with the program and curled up against Victor, burying his head in Victor's shoulder this time. Figuring Doug needed reassurance and time to adjust to the idea, Victor just held him, crooning comfort and gently massaging tense muscles. After a few minutes, Victor's holding and stroking transmuted into nuzzling and fondling. Doug rolled over again, flat on his back this time, arms and legs spread like a snow angel. Like a human sacrifice, like… "Jesus Christ, Doug. This is sex, not penance. Could you maybe act like it isn't such a trial? You Catholic or what?"

"I just want to make it up to you. It's my fault you got shot in the leg. I thought this would be a way to make it right between us again."

Victor continued to pet and pat Doug's pliant body as he considered this. Could he do it? Would it put them on an even keel again? He caressed the ladder of Doug's ribs, noting absently how much definition he'd gained since they'd first met at the gym. The situation wasn't simple. He palmed a pelvic bone. It wasn't straightforward: an eye for an eye, a ex-boyfriend for an ex-wife. He ringed Doug's navel with his middle finger. This was…complicated. Confusing. Lost in thought, he stroked Doug's erection a little faster.

Whoa there! Erection? Doug had a hard-on? That meant Doug was enjoying this. At least a little.

Giving it more attention now, Victor swiped a thumb across the head, feeling just the faintest trace of moisture there.

Hmmm. Usually the only thing Victor liked uncut was his movies, but he could really get to like this. He tugged at Doug's foreskin gently, eliciting a sigh.

Did Doug like the image of himself as suffering? Was he into painful sex? Or did the whole penance thing give him an excuse to be doing what he really wanted? Victor certainly hoped it was the latter. He covered Doug's balls with his free hand and gave a little squeeze. Good. Heavier breathing, microscopic lift of the hips. He squeezed harder; the absence of sound or movement was telling. He squeezed harder still. "Victor." Doug's hand closed on his wrist and dragged it away.

"Too much, Doug?"

"It's rather uncomfortable, Victor. Do some men…? Do you?"

"Enjoy pain? Yeah, some do. Do I? No way. I like things…gentle but firm." He moved his hand back to test Doug's dick again; semi-hard now, but making a reprise under Victor's gentle but firm massage. Maybe…

But Doug wasn't relaxing. He was still strung like a violin wire: coiled, vibrating, and ready to snap. There was probably only one way to resolve this, and Victor made his decision. "Hand me the baby oil, Doug, and roll over on your stomach. We're going to finish what we started before the cable guy so rudely interrupted us."

Despite his directive to Doug, it was Victor who found the baby oil in the folds of the sheets. He waited for Doug to lie back down, then positioned himself over Doug's firm ass, a knee on each side and his own hard-on nestled warmly in the yielding and slightly sweaty crevice. He rubbed himself up and down a few times and almost gave in then and there to the temptations of the flesh, but he managed to get a grip by getting a grip and squeezing hard, and continued with his plan.

Victor drizzled oil between Doug's shoulder blades and along his spine, and began to stroke and caress his prostrate body.

Doug groaned loudly.

"Yeah, baby. That's it."

"Oh, Victor."

"Let me hear how much you want this."

"Oooohhhh, Victor."

"How much you're enjoying this."

"Ahhh, Victor! Victor! Victor! VICTOR!"

Who knew Doug could come from a backrub? Victor told his own hard-on to just suck it up as he snuggled against the almost comatose Doug and settled down for the night. Some things were worth waiting for.

He drifted off to sleep humming the old Supremes hit "Can't Hurry Love."

DELIGHT AT THE END OF THE TUNNEL

Gummy eyes. Gummy mouth. What the fuck time is it?

Victor knocked something unidentified to the floor as he fumbled to press the really big button on the clock radio. The clock, a gift from Doug when they'd first set up housekeeping together several weeks before, projected the time onto the ceiling in huge digits: 6:30. Too early. Back to sleep. He snuggled up against Doug and dozed a bit.

"That's six thirty p.m., Victor." Doug stretched magnificently, popping an entire rhythm section of vertebrae. "We slept the better part of the day away."

"We were up all night." Victor spoke without moving anything: not lips, nor lungs, nor larynx.

"Now we've thrown our sleep patterns off and we'll be up all this night as well."

"Pizza for breakfast," was Victor's contribution to the conversation before he drifted back to dreamland, visions of fairies, sugarplum or otherwise, dancing in his head.

Victor finally surfaced again an hour later. He struggled out from under the covers; they'd twisted them up pretty good when they got home the previous evening, er, morning. Whatever. Doug had been all pumped from his first-ever active role in a takedown — unless you counted taking out Veronica Amorotique over a year ago, but Victor's leg hurt when he thought of her so he didn't.

Doug and his newly assembled team of freelance forensic accountants and computer experts had been of great assistance last night when Victor's police division had raided the premises of an illegal online casino ring. After a preliminary review of some of the confiscated files and computers, Doug and his merry band were sure they could prove beyond a shadow of a doubt not only that the gang was running a gaming facility without a license, but that they were also big into money laundering. Victor was delighted with the opportunity to work with his partner, and at how smoothly it had all gone down — not a shot fired, scarcely a scuffle. It appeared that computer criminal types weren't into fisticuffs, as Doug would have said.

Although last night had been something of a non-event to someone with Victor's experience — and he meant the bust, not the sex — he'd been so relieved he'd had an equally large supply of adrenalin to work off, and they certainly had.

He wrapped his sarong around his waist, suddenly shy with his new housemate, and exited the bedroom for the living room. Apparently modesty was a moot point anyway, since Doug and Jack were AWOL. Victor made a quick check for Jack's leash and the fanny pack that held plastic bags, flashlight, and other necessities of doody duty. Since they were also gone, Doug was obviously walking Jack. Victor headed for the shower.

✖ ✖ ✖

The bathroom door opened, spewing steam and Victor into the living room. He toweled most of the excess water from his hair as he headed to the kitchen for coffee. It must have been there awhile and was kind of stale, but beggars couldn't be choosers. He sat at the table with the morning paper to distract him from the harsh taste.

He was just finished cup number one when Doug and Jack put in an appearance. Jack bounded over to him with a shit-eating grin on his muzzle.

"Hey!" He pushed ineffectually at Jack, who was wiping his muzzle on Victor's sweatpants under the feeble guise of affection. "He roll in anything, dead or otherwise?"

"Not that I'm aware of, Victor, although I did detect the odor of early spring pollen as we came up the hallway. I do believe he's finally learned some impulse control."

"Pollen, eh?" Jack and Victor both sneezed, trading body fluids in equal proportions. Victor sniffled, then sniffed as best he could. "What's in the bag?"

"Coffee and egg sandwiches from the diner. Levon asked me to convey his good wishes to you."

"You mean he said 'tell that ol' queer hey', right? How's he like flipping burgers for your old neighbor?"

"He is grateful to you for 'hooking him up' with the part-time job while he continues his studies. Mr. Nbizzlemeiner says Levon is a very reliable employee. And he brings in a lot of business."

"Yeah. The diner's the only place that's open all night so all the kids head there after the clubs close." Victor yawned. "I remember the days when I could party all night and into the next day. He still seein' Delroy?"

"Apparently so, as he asked if we were interested in double-dating sometime. I believe he feels very attached to you, thanks to your patience and wisdom."

"Wisdom smisdom. I just calls 'em as I gaydar 'em." He took the last sip of the nearly cold coffee in his mug. "Oh, yetch. This is foul." He tilted the cup to get the last drops where all the sugar congealed.

"I don't believe coffee ages very well, so you may wish to dump our current pot." Doug handed the bag to Victor, which pretty much made everything right in Victor's world. He carefully inched the foam cup around until the little drinking hole was directly beneath his lips and took a cautious sip. Ah. Coffee. Food. A terrific boyfriend. A successful, incident-free bust and another entire day off before he had to return to work. Could it get any better than this? A sip and a sigh. Heaven. He hummed a happy tune and realized that something was indeed missing.

"Put on some tunes, will you, Doug?"

Doug ambled over to the living room, crouching sexily to look through their massive, combined CD collection. "Did you have anything in particular in mind?"

"Put on that piano guy, whatsisface, Rock Man Enough. He's right next to Rock Visine."

Doug tsked and shook his head. Since he had his back to the dining alcove, it was impossible for Victor to tell if he was pissed or amused at the wordplay. Victor always entertained himself, though.

Doug rose without having selected a CD. "Actually, Victor, if you're in the mood for classical, I'd like to play the new CD I bought on Thursday. It's Bach's "Cello-Suiten" performed by Mstislav Rostropovich. I believe you'll enjoy it."

Victor walked over to the three bursting CD racks. "We've got to stop buying CDs, Doug. There's no more space." He eyed the wobbly racks with distrust.

"Don't be silly, Victor." Doug returned to the living room with the new CD. "There's always room for cello."

There was a momentary pause, then both men began laughing at the terrible, terrible play on words.

When they'd calmed down enough, they meticulously mopped up the coffee-egg sandwich mélange from the entertainment unit to the excellent accompanying sounds of Bach.

※ ※ ※

Later, seated side by side on the sofa, first Victor yawned hugely, then Doug followed suit, covering his mouth, of course. "It's one in the morning, Victor. I think we should go to bed now to attempt to re-regulate our sleep patterns."

Victor was just getting into a Bruce Lee movie he'd been meaning to see for about three decades.

"So let me get this straight." Victor muted the volume and watched Doug struggle with an incipient grin. "I can stay out here in the living room and watch this movie or I can turn off the TV and go to bed with the sexiest man in Canada." He sat forward and rubbed his chin thoughtfully. "Let me think about this." He leaned back and unmuted the sound, not too concerned that he might have missed vital dialogue. Just how far along could a plot be moved by *hi-yahhh*?

Doug sat a moment longer, then stood and positioned himself directly between Victor and the television set. "I wonder, Victor, if there's anything I can do to assist you in making this significant decision." The words were bland, but Doug's tone was husky, sexy, and his eyes were hooded and dark.

"I can't see anything at the moment," Victor deadpanned, feigning interest in seeing around him. "Can you do anything about that?"

"I can certainly try, Victor. Do let me know if you like what you see." Slowly, sensually and still charmingly self-conscious, Doug stroked his hand up his own chest, unbuttoning from the top down when he got to the collar. Victor found his breath quickening as Doug, finished with the buttons, drew the shirttail free of his jeans and peeled the shirt unhurriedly away from his well-defined torso.

"Nice six-pack, Doug. You must work out."

"I have a great training partner. He's shown me all sorts of interesting exercises." Victor shifted on the couch. "I feel it's only right to reward him."

"But we just had Christmas a couple of months ago." Victor toyed with the drawstring on the old sweats he'd donned after his shower.

"But we do have a Christmas tree." Doug spun lazily in place until he faced the TV, which Victor now shut off, arcing the signal around him. Doug went into a double-bicep pose, causing a pine-tree-shaped indentation to appear in the small of his back, with a freckle instead of a star on the top. He peered over his shoulder, looking suddenly shy. "Or so I'm told."

Pushing up off the couch, hard-on preceding him, Victor brought himself up behind his posing boyfriend and traced the triangular impression at the base of Doug's spine. Doug tensed, then relaxed as Victor's warm hands sketched his upper body, grip closing on one rock-hard bicep.

Letting go, Victor backed off a step or two to better admire the view, ordering, "Now give me a lat spread." Doug dropped his fists from above his shoulders to dig his thumbs into his waist. He took a couple of runs at it, but eventually drew a deep breath and spread his lats like wings. Victor thought of caterpillars turning into butterflies. Of ugly ducklings becoming beautiful swans. Of angels fallen from heaven. Of how beautiful Doug was and how lucky Victor was to have him.

Doug wouldn't win any bodybuilding contests, but he was in the best shape of his life and looked amazing. Victor loved him for it, but then again, Victor had begun to love him back when he was one dumbbell heavier, couldn't manage to run a mile, and believed himself straight. Victor felt a wave of warmth traverse him; he'd still love Doug even when he'd lost his muscles, his hair, his eyesight, his ability to go at it for hours...

Stepping up behind Doug again, he began to lick and kiss his broad back. Gradually Doug relaxed the pose and Victor worked his way round to the front, making sure all the major muscle groups had a good work out: tris, bis, delts, traps, pecs, nipples. He was just trying to decide if he should go straight for the quads and back to the glutes or get in a little lip action when Doug asked seductively, "Are there any other poses you'd like me to do for you?"

"Well, since you *pose* the question, I'd like to put you on a pedestal, Adonis — something soft and horizontal, maybe." Victor grabbed his hand and dragged him to the bedroom, darting back out to put on something Latin and instrumental — no distracting lyrics, just a good beat. He shed his ratty old T-shirt and moved to the doorway to do a little posing himself.

Six-pack met killer abs as Doug leaned up against him, grinding his hips against Victor once, twice, three times while holding his gaze, lips curving a little, just out of reach. Victor dove for that sweet mouth twice, but Doug was teasing, playing hard to get. Victor grinned and leaned back against the doorframe. Doug would come to him when he was ready. He wasn't going anywhere.

He wrapped one hand around Doug's tricep, holding onto the doorframe for support with the other. He widened his stance a bit and Doug thrust again, shimmying his hips a little for effect. The first thrusts had obviously been for Doug, but this one was definitely directed at Victor, who hissed appreciatively, sucking air in between his tightly clenched teeth.

Victor released the arm he'd been clutching, and ran his hand down Doug's back until it rested on that firm ass. He squeezed, and was rewarded with another little shimmy: Doug had a very sensitive backside. Victor squeezed again. He just loved this, his time with Doug, his playtime with Doug: wordplay, byplay, foreplay. He didn't think he'd ever been happier, ever smiled as often, ever laughed so much. He felt like laughing right then, so he did.

Doug drew back, looking confused, but smiling a little, too. "What's so funny, Victor? Not still the cello reference?"

"Nah. Yeah, that too. Just…this. You. Me. Us. You're fun. We're good. I'm happy."

Now Doug smiled too, reaching out to trace the lines of Victor's grin, first with his fingertips, slightly calloused from long hours at the computer, then with his tongue, which Victor was surprised wasn't calloused from the long hours of necking they'd put in over the last few months, especially since they'd moved in together.

Victor tickled Doug's lips in return, knowing he didn't actually like it. Doug pulled back again, pushing Victor's hand away and giving him a half-assed stern look. Then Victor leaned in and nipped the itchy spot, and got a real stern look.

"I'm going to have to teach you some manners, Victor Brighton." Quicksilver-fast, Victor found himself gone from the doorway and facedown on the bed, head where his feet should be, with Doug straddling his back and yanking at his sweatpants. Victor made the weakest of attempts to throw off his assailant, assuming Doug just wanted to finish undressing him. He felt hot breath on his ass and relaxed slightly. Lips and tongue, moving over his cheeks and running down the furrow, following breath. Oh, God, was Doug going to…? He'd never done that to Victor, to anyone, he'd said, after Victor had done it to him. Victor tried to relax, not to clench, and nearly jumped out of his skin when Doug bit him instead. Hard.

"Ow! Hey! Ow!" Doug lightened up a bit but kept on biting Victor's ass, and, like most everything else Doug did to Victor, it quickly got good to him. "Ow!" became "Oh!" then *"Ooooo!"* Doug varied the harsh teeth with gentle swipes of his tongue, the contrast delightful.

He remembered vaguely that he was being mock-punished for some transgression. He'd have to remember to transgress more often. He figured he was leaking by now and gave a bit of thought to the just-cleaned bedspread, then lost all rational thought when slick fingers toyed with his hole. *Jeez. Jeez. Jeez.* It felt so good.

Panting, nearly beside himself, Victor felt his sweats being removed completely, Doug having un-straddled him to do so. He was naked except for his formerly white sweatsocks. Unforgivable. He'd have to take those off…later. He felt Doug position himself behind him and rose up on his knees. Doug entered him smoothly, having taken care of all the details like lube and condom while Victor basked in pleasure.

Entry was always a little painful for Victor, and brought him back to reality for a moment. Knowing this, Doug was always slow and gentle at the outset. He'd agonized over telling Doug about the initial pain because he'd had such a hard time convincing Doug to do it at all. Doug was so scared of hurting Victor as he himself had been hurt way back when, that it had taken some time and a huge amount of patience to convince his lover that he really, really liked it once they got going. There'd been some begging too, he recalled.

Trust had prevailed. He'd been honest with Doug, both about the mechanics of it and about how it was worth it, and eventually Doug had given it a shot. Victor giggled at his own pun. Doug must have figured the giggling indicated the first act was over; he upped the pace a notch.

Oh, yeah. Good. Getting good. Victor reached for his re-burgeoning erection, only to have his hand grabbed and drawn away. *Oh. Okay.* He needed his hands to support himself so he didn't hit his head on the foot rail, anyway. The momentum of Doug's pistoning had moved them further toward the end of the bed. and Victor found himself draped over the brass footboard, which was great since it gave him leverage to counterthrust, thrust, counterthrust, thrust, thrust, thrust. *Oh yeah, baby. Give it to me.*

The pace reached lightning speed and crescendoed with a shudder, with Doug collapsing across his back. Victor assumed he was panting, but couldn't hear anything over the sound of his own heartbeat. He could just barely make out the words Doug was saying, though. They sounded very much like "I love you, Victor."

Victor was a good man. A kind man. A patient man. He gave Doug a good three minutes to recover before he took Doug's right hand and placed it on his erection. Doug circled it loosely, giving a half-hearted squeeze before just sort of holding it gently.

Victor gave him another thirty seconds, then thrust up into the loose circle of fingers a couple of times. Doug was obviously misunderstanding here. *What?* First Doug had stopped him from giving himself a friendly helping hand, and now he wasn't doing it either. Well, somebody better get handy real soon! He thrust one more time for good measure.

Doug gave him a friendly squeeze, a little more in control of his muscles this time, then removed his hand. *Huh?*

He left the room for a few moments, heading for the bathroom, returning without the condom.

He re-joined Victor on the bed. They were still wrong way up, so he snagged a pillow with one foot and forced it under Victor's head.

Comfortable, shmomfortable. Somebody'd better get Victor off and soon. It wasn't going to jack itself!

Doug rolled up against him and the kissing started all over again. Long moments passed, lots of kissing and fondling. Victor thrust against Doug's nice, hard belly, being a little careful not to involve Doug's softening dick, which could be overly sensitive so soon after coming.

Victor was getting more and more worked up. Doug reached between them, stroking his thighs, balls, cock, but not hard enough, not satisfying him or even bringing him any closer to relief.

He was just about to say something coherent, something more than the things he'd been saying all along: Oh, God; Jeez; that feels good; you feel so good; I love you; do that again.

Doug reached behind him, evidently searching for something, then finding it, handed Victor the bottle of Wet and a strip of condoms.

There could be no mistaking his meaning, but Victor still asked if he was sure. Doug assured him he was, that it was time, and that he was okay with it.

"You're not just doing this 'cause you feel you owe me or anything, are you?" Victor cared deeply about Doug's answer, even as he tugged a condom on over his fingers and smeared lube on it — Doug liked things better if they were neat. Doug's response was to roll away from him so his back was toward Victor.

This part wasn't entirely new to them. What man could resist the idea of a whole new pleasure spot he'd previously been unaware of? Of course Doug had been skeptical at first, but he'd done the research and knew it wasn't just some Victor thing. And had nearly gone through the roof the first time Victor had gently touched his prostate. He'd been a bit embarrassed by his whole reaction; he'd never quite overcome the prim Victorian upbringing he'd acquired through being raised by caregivers two generations out of step with the times. But he'd loved it and on a couple of occasions, he'd let Victor boldly go where almost no man had gone before — first with fingers, and later, after much coaxing, with tongue, as well.

And Victor did boldly go now, easing in, stroking, stoking, caressing, slicking and stretching, mixing pleasure with practicality, sensuality with slicking up.

He slid the condom off his fingers, careful to drop it into the handy wastebasket, or near enough. He reached over Doug's hip for a little exploration, and found that Doug had indeed rejoined the land of the living, a brand spanking new erection pointed toward the bedroom wall.

Victor was glad of unslick fingers as he rolled a new condom down over his impatient and leaking cock. It deserved a big reward for waiting so long. He'd been contemplating the best position for Doug's first time — second first time, that is. He considered face-to-face since that hockey asshole had only ever taken him from the back, but that was more awkward and Doug did get embarrassed about the more messy parts, so he decided spooning was good. Spooning was great, and he pulled himself up close, closer, closest to Doug's back. Ass, meet dick: dick, ass. He reached behind him, lifted up a bit and yanked away the covers that had rucked up between them. Nothing was going to come between them now.

He just let his dick rest in the shadowy crevice of Doug's ass for a moment, stroking Doug's arm and trying to gauge his state of mind.

"This is it, Doug. You 'bout ready there?"

"All systems go, Victor," Doug joked, voice hardly quavering at all.

A firm nod and Victor took himself in hand, bringing the head squarely against Doug's slick opening. *Houston, we have contact.* He pushed a little, not surprised to feel Doug tense up. He didn't have to wait long for Doug to relax and even make a tentative little thrust back against him, impaling another couple of centimeters.

Victor groaned and pushed a bit more, feeling Doug's heart pounding under his palm. He didn't check Doug's erection again, figuring it would only embarrass Doug by its absence. Besides, it wouldn't really be indicative of whether Doug was enjoying it or not; he probably wouldn't at this point, although Victor had made it as good for him as he possibly could once they got going.

He listened for the sound of Doug's breathing, but it would be heavy whether he was enjoying it or just scared. He'd just have to trust Doug to tell him if it wasn't working, just as Doug was trusting him to make it good, or stop when he said so.

He tried another little thrust and found he couldn't. He was all the way in. When had that happened? He'd been so focused on Doug's vital signs that he hadn't even noticed the gentle slip and slide of his cock until it had come to rest, cradled tightly in Doug's ass.

Wow! This was…This was… *Wow!* Victor tried rocking a little bit, and the third time Doug rocked with him. Then he got the beat and rocked against him, mirroring their thrust and counterthrust of a few minutes ago. Victor began to pull back further with each thrust, pushing in again firmly, but not roughly. He'd fucked harder, but never better; he moved his hand down to Doug's belly, pushing against the firm abs and feeling more confident. He rose up on one elbow and started to thrust in earnest.

"You," he gasped, "okay?" *Oh yeah, like that. Just like that.*

"Fine. Victor." The words rushed out between groans. "And you?"

"Never," he groaned, "better." He drew a deep breath and mantra'd: "Never ever ever better." And that was it for conversation as he felt his orgasm overtake him. Swift rhythmic thrusts, a staccato burst of short, hard strokes and he cried out, something about love maybe, as he filled the condom.

There was nuzzling, cuddling, endearments and various whispered health checks consisting of repeated "You okay?" and similar questions, until Doug finally snapped at Victor that he was fine. Magic over, for that night anyway.

There were yawns and stretches and a reminder to Jack that he had an entire couch in the other room, and the spooning position made a chaste reappearance and, eventually, so did sleep.

Victor was almost sure just before he dropped off to sleep that Doug reached over him to kiss his cheek and whisper something about love and trust and thank you.

Or maybe he just dreamed it.

ABOUT THE AUTHOR

After tossing yet another commercial bestseller aside unfinished (and deepening the dent in the wall), Storm Grant declared, "I too can write this badly!" Apparently she doesn't write too badly after all. Just a few years later, she's contracted stories to a number of publishers, both electronic and print.

Storm is a board member of the Toronto chapter of the RWA. She holds a degree in business and has spent three decades working in marketing and administration. Her writing experience includes commercial copywriting, as well as fiction. She lives in Toronto, Canada, in a rather messy house with one husband and a miscellany of rescued pets.

Follow Storm's life and writing career at her blog:

http://storm-grant.livejournal.com;

Email her at:

storm.grant@gmail.com.

Fiction that's pretty, witty, straight and gay!

THE TREVOR PROJECT

The Trevor Project operates the only nationwide, around-the-clock crisis and suicide prevention helpline for lesbian, gay, bisexual, transgender and questioning youth. Every day, The Trevor Project saves lives though its free and confidential helpline, its website and its educational services. If you or a friend are feeling lost or alone call The Trevor Helpline. If you or a friend are feeling lost, alone, confused or in crisis, please call The Trevor Helpline. You'll be able to speak confidentially with a trained counselor 24/7.

The Trevor Helpline: 866-488-7386

On the Web: http://www.thetrevorproject.org/

THE GAY MEN'S DOMESTIC VIOLENCE PROJECT

Founded in 1994, The Gay Men's Domestic Violence Project is a grassroots, non-profit organization founded by a gay male survivor of domestic violence and developed through the strength, contributions and participation of the community. The Gay Men's Domestic Violence Project supports victims and survivors through education, advocacy and direct services. Understanding that the serious public health issue of domestic violence is not gender specific, we serve men in relationships with men, regardless of how they identify, and stand ready to assist them in navigating through abusive relationships.

GMDVP Helpline: 800.832.1901

On the Web: http://gmdvp.org/

THE GAY & LESBIAN ALLIANCE AGAINST DEFAMATION/GLAAD EN ESPAÑOL

The Gay & Lesbian Alliance Against Defamation (GLAAD) is dedicated to promoting and ensuring fair, accurate and inclusive representation of people and events in the media as a means of eliminating homophobia and discrimination based on gender identity and sexual orientation.

On the Web: http://www.glaad.org/

GLAAD en español:

http://www.glaad.org/espanol/bienvenido.php

If you're a GLBT and questioning student heading off to university, should know that there are resources on campus for you. Here's just a sample:

US Local GLBT college campus organizations
> http://dv-8.com/resources/us/local/campus.html

GLBT Scholarship Resources
> http://tinyurl.com/6fx9v6

Syracuse University
> http://lgbt.syr.edu/

Texas A&M
> http://glbt.tamu.edu/

Tulane University
> http://www.oma.tulane.edu/LGBT/Default.htm

University of Alaska
> http://www.uaf.edu/agla/

University of California, Davis
> http://lgbtrc.ucdavis.edu/

University of California, San Francisco
> http://lgbt.ucsf.edu/

University of Colorado
> http://www.colorado.edu/glbtrc/

University of Florida
> http://www.dso.ufl.edu/multicultural/lgbt/

University of Hawai'i, Mānoa
> http://manoa.hawaii.edu/lgbt/

University of Utah
> http://www.sa.utah.edu/lgbt/

University of Virginia
> http://www.virginia.edu/deanofstudents/lgbt/

Vanderbilt University
> http://www.vanderbilt.edu/lgbtqi/

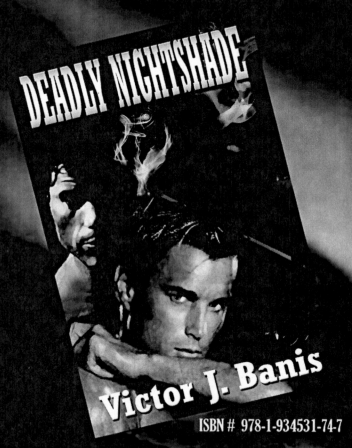

Stimulate yourself.
READ.
www.manloveromance.com
THE HOTTEST M/M EROTIC AUTHORS & WEBSITES ON THE NET

Printed in the United States
144811LV00001B/7/P